The Dance of a Sham

The Dance of a Sham

Paul Emond

Translated by Marlon Jones

DALKEY ARCHIVE PRESS
Champaign / London / Dublin

Originally published in French as *La Danse du fumiste* by Éditions Jacques Antoine (become Les Éperonniers), Brussels, 1979

Copyright © 2012 Communauté française de Belgique, coll. Espace Nord.

Translation copyright © 2013 by Marlon Jones

First edition, 2014

Library of Congress Cataloging-in-Publication Data

Emond, Paul.
    [Danse du fumiste. English]
    The dance of a sham / Paul Emond; translated by Marlon Jones. -- 1st ed.

    pages cm
    ISBN 978-1-62897-032-6 (pbk. :alk. paper)
    I. Jones, Marlon, translator. II. Title.
    PQ2665.M66D3613 2014
    843'.914--dc23

                    2014001182

Partially funded by a grant from the Illinois Arts Council, a state agency

This translation was published with the support of Ministère de la Fédération Wallonie-Bruxelles

www.dalkeyarchive.com

Cover: design and composition by Mikhail Iliatov;
Printed on permanent/durable acid-free paper

To myself,
very sincerely.

THAT GUY TALKED like a book, he could chat like breathing, I can tell you right now he wasn't the type to make a lot of slips of the tongue, the type who needs to waffle his words back and forth ten times before saying something, everyone would stop to listen to him and if he'd gone into politics he'd be a Secretary of State right now, I even think when he started telling a story he didn't know exactly what he was going to say, often he must have just started talking for the sheer pleasure of talking, and the story just followed naturally in stride, he had such eloquence, such a gift of the gab, and crafty as a monkey to boot, you never needed to tell him twice what was going on, plus he had his own ideas about everything, he knew it all, people liked him because he was always up for anything, the life of every party, it's true that back then people knew how to live, we had heart and character, as they say, and manners and quibbling weren't our department, when we got some urge we'd charge straight ahead without stopping or turning back, if that guy took it into his head to widen his field he would have killed his neighbor to do it, we could drink all night and stay up the whole next day fresh as a daisy, occasionally we even woke up in a ditch, that's where the police found me one time and brought me home, my mom was shouting, haven't you brought enough shame on us already, eh, haven't you, and she was shouting so loudly the police were more scared than I was, they cleared out really quick, apologizing for the inconvenience but my mom wasn't even listening, I was the one she was after, you see, and she went on with her litany, aren't you ashamed, don't you feel any shame, I've got to say, that was a serious bit of merrymaking, I'd been out with my buddy for three days and we went to every bar in a seven-mile radius, I'd even lost him at some point without realizing, he must have stayed with some girl because you couldn't imagine the success he had with the young ladies, he'd serve them up his finest speeches, hot, just the right word to get them giggling and he had a knack even with the most reluctant ones, they never had time to get bored with him, he was never one to beat around the bush, my method's a straight line, he'd say, cutting the air with his hand, but once it was over there was no question of sentimental primness, it was more of a hello, can I slide into your bunk, drop my little men and see you later, he had to have all of them, a blond then a brunette, one after the other, he was the champion of hanky-panky and proud of it but they knew what he was like and didn't hold it against him, not usually, except one who wanted to kill him because she got pregnant, he claimed he wasn't the father, no way I'm going to be the pigeon here, he told me, I think there's somebody who's been hanging out with her, she came looking for him, well she found him in the end, because he was laying low, he'd decided he'd rather not stay at home with all this going on, she's told him it was his baby, that he couldn't leave her alone like this but he just laughed, if you think I'm going to fall for your tall tales, I know exactly what's going on, I'm not an idiot, then she grabbed the kettle off the stove and he got it right in the face with the boiling water, he was howling like a skunk, filthy bitch, I'm blind and you're going to pay for this, he was rolling on the floor, he even thought he should go to the hospital for treatment, but he stayed in bed for a few days with compresses on his face and afterwards you couldn't see anything, that guy was sturdy, the girl moved away, people said later she died during a failed abortion but they say all kinds of things, who knows what's true or false in all the rumors you hear, it's like all the stuff they said about me around the village when I did two months of prison, we were walking around in the next town over and it's true we'd been drinking a bit, so since we were broke, we thought we'd swipe this old lady's bag as she walked by, there weren't a lot of people around, it seemed like a straight forward grab, all we had to do was snatch the bag and take off, but unfortunately that was one tough old lady, hands like steel hooks, she was holding her property with all her might and yelling thief, thief in a piercing voice, my buddy hit her to make her shut up but some people came over and he ran off, there were two or three people holding me, I couldn't get away, then a cop came and I got a heck of a beating at the station, when I got out of prison two months later, my buddy'd disappeared, he didn't come back until much later, when people had forgotten the whole thing, and I've got to say, it was the right move since he was the one who'd hit the old lady, he could have gone down for a long time, I liked it when he started telling stories, or just thinking out loud, he could talk like that for hours, he'd say I know I'm a talker but I can't help it, chatting keeps me alive, and the reason he liked me so much was because he knew I was his best listener, it's true that once he got started I could have listened forever, I would have followed him to the ends of the earth, and we'd take some fantastical paths, I'd follow all the way, then he'd take the bit between his teeth, his phrases came galloping along and you had to hang on tight, he'd cut his turns at an ever more frenzied pace, I'll tell you some hodge, then tell you some podge, I start my stories hither and send them over thither, I didn't let go for a second, I was always there listening to him tirelessly, I was like that guy on his donkey following a half-crazy knight around, I've got to say, my imagination always liked to wander, when I was a kid I'd spend days at a time thinking of my real parents, my parents from town, one day they'd come and get me in a big black limousine, obviously I was just in custody with my fake parents, the ones in the village, for some strange reason that I would find out later, that was the only explanation for my fake parents disliking me so much, and yelling at me all the time, anyway I'd figured out right away I had nothing in common with those people, and I didn't see my dad much, he went to work early in the morning and came home exhausted in the evening, and sometimes he didn't even come home at all and my mother would gripe, she thought it was suspicious the way he always had some excuse for spending the night in town, some months it happened a bit too often, and when my dad got back there'd be a real blow-up, especially if she found proof, a little handkerchief left at the bottom of his satchel, or a suspicious odor on his clothes, I can smell tart, she'd scream, I know exactly where you've been hanging around again, Lord what did I do to deserve a man like this, an absolute good-for-nothing, family dramas always make for vivid memories, like the guy who was nearly engaged to my cousin, he'd come over every Sunday to play the sweetheart and fondle his Dulcinea like an

honorable squire, he brought chocolates for my aunt, who thought
he was very sophisticated, and my uncle had already loaned him
some money to start a wholesale coffee business, he already called
him son-in-law, and the fiancé knew how to set the mood, he had a
really dry sense of humor and the family made a pretty sight when
they went on their Sunday afternoon walk, the lovebirds walked arm
in arm, the parents followed along watching them tenderly, not long
afterwards they made all the arrangements for the wedding, I remember it was supposed to be in July, one fine Sunday the fiancé
didn't show up and they thought he was sick, but they never heard
from him again and couldn't find a trace of him afterwards, it finally
turned out he'd moved away, he went to live far away with his own
family, his wife and three children, because the fiancé was already
married, so it was a crushing disgrace for my cousin and her parents,
the fallout affected our whole family, and my mom said a man like
that deserves to be hanged, that Al Capone was a choirboy compared
to him, that really impressed me, I'd heard that when Al Capone
gunned down his enemies with a tommy gun, he'd go up to the bodies smoking a huge cigar and nonchalantly shake ash onto their faces,
it was dreadful and elegant at the same time and I imagined the fake
fiancé savoring his cigar and looking down at my aunt's body at this
feet, I should tell you my aunt was very fat and extremely respectable
and I was really frightened of her, sometimes I'd go to her house during vacations and if I didn't behave myself at the table she'd slap my
hand, so to drop ash on her body was an incredible sacrilege, one day
after that painful story they came to visit my parents, my cousin
cried all through dinner and everybody kept telling her the guy was
a scoundrel and she was a poor dear, and the poor dear entered a
convent about a year later, apparently she died fairly recently, but
you know I'm not in close touch with the family anymore, everybody goes his separate way in life, you can't be in two places at once
and it's true that you're better off counting on yourself than on your
family, my buddy often explained that if he'd listened to his parents
he would have ended up just some pigeon to pluck, he'd realized

once and for all that you can divide people into two categories, the toughs and the pigeons, and you've got to make sure you're with the toughs, just think, with them I'd be like Job on his dung-heap right now, they spent all their time preaching to me about work and honesty, and we know where that leads, and also they were always over at the priest's house and I had to serve mass and go to catechism sessions, but when it came to catechism my buddy's resentment was a little too bitter, it actually wasn't that bad, the girls came too, when we did, we all tried to get them to notice us and we'd see who could pull the best faces, showing off, gesturing towards the exit, and the good priest was concentrating too hard on the story he was telling to notice our antics, his stories were as dull as ditchwater but he went to a lot of trouble trying to be persuasive, there was one girl I liked a lot, her name was Marie-Ange, angel, I always thought it was an extraordinary name, she married a guy from town who worked in insurance, I heard she has several children now, I also heard she got really fat and is very unhappy at home, sometimes I dream I meet her and she's still beautiful the way she used to be, and then she becomes the great love of my life, I tell myself about all kinds of adventures that happen to us, I have to say I always take great pleasure in fixing myself up this little theater, my little continuous show, I cook up my own style of existence, which is extraordinary, away from the day-to-day monotony, at first Marie-Ange couldn't stand me, and all I could think about was taking a tumble in the hay with her, she got off with all the boys in the area, she was known for it, but with me, she kept me at arm's length, don't touch, she'd say if I got too close, it's too high quality for you, I never knew why but she called me the bastard, here comes the bastard again, hovering around me, she'd sneer, I was her scapegoat, every night I'd dream about her, that I was stroking her, I wanted her so badly I'd holler in my sleep, then at the last second she'd slip away and I'd wake up and it was back to square one, my buddy had told me about this tribe of toughs in antiquity that attacked another tribe to steal their women, they'd killed all the men and taken the prettiest ones, and I imagined myself leading my tribe and raiding Marie-Ange's village, after the last war a man who'd gone off to fight and they'd thought had died came back to the village, after so many months with no news his wife had gotten together with someone else, so when the soldier got home he didn't find her there, the neighbors told him the truth, he didn't say anything, but he went over to the house where the other guy lived and went in, there was a gunshot and the next second he came out, pulling his wife by the hair, the poor thing was screaming with fright, there was a trial but he got acquitted, he claimed the other guy had tried to kill him and he'd only been defending himself, and you have to understand he'd become a national hero in the war and court didn't push too hard, his wife came back to live with him as if nothing had happened and the most stunning part of the story was that a few years later he got fed up and one fine day he left her and went off to become a sailor, I don't think she ever saw him again, one time my buddy and I met some sailors in town, we had a lot to drink all together and they kept bragging more and more, claiming they had girlfriends in every port in the world, with the charm of their uniform, all the pretty ones flung themselves into their arms, my buddy got fed up in the end, he wanted to tell his success stories, but the sailors were so drunk they wouldn't give him a chance to talk, there was no way things weren't going to turn nasty, and people started shoving each other, it was quite a show with chairs flying all over the place, the manager called the police, the sailors cleared out in a hurry, so did we, actually, but I think those guys were looking to avoid any contact with the police, they'd been on leave in the area for two or three days and they already had a really bad reputation, and the thing is, my buddy told me the next day, you always need to watch out with foreigners, when my buddy said something he liked to start the first sentence with, you see, and sometimes just after saying those two words he'd stop for a second as if he wanted to savor them, he'd watch me to see them sink in, to see if I really did see, or rather if it got me in the right frame of mind to see, it was a way to get me in a state of perfect communication, a way to dominate me, and it's true he was a bit of a wizard, he managed to breathe a sort of magic into those two words, all it took was him saying them and immediately I felt I could hear anything, he'd say you see and it opened my intelligence, right then I found myself riding alongside him, and then we could keep galloping all day, his stories never stopped, they went on and on, there was always some new development, an unexpected event, a sudden murder, then off we'd go and I can tell you there was no question of changing horses mid-river, you had to take the whole trip in one stretch, however long it was, what was weird is that he claimed he never dreamed when he was asleep, I'm sure it wasn't true but it was part of his persona, you see, he'd say, when I doze it hits me like an axe, I sleep intensely and I've got no time for dreams, I'm the prince of the dormice, maybe all those stories he told actually never did come disturb his sleep, maybe his dreams were full of silence, big, peaceful dreams like fields of snow, when he was asleep his face looked like a child's, he'd curl up in the fetal position and he looked defenseless, he lost all his arrogance, lost that alpha male look of his, constantly on the lookout, no more snapping for no reason, just a deep, silent pause, there was a guy who lived near the village who never talked much even when he came to the bars to get drunk from time to time, he was a chatless type, as they say around here, his name was Victor and he'd been one of the last shepherds in the area, because you know after the war all the old professions disappeared really quickly, he had a little house in the middle of the fields, it was raised slightly, so you could see it from far away, he must not have had much money, Victor, sometimes he'd lend a hand on the farms in the area to earn enough to get by, but people in the village said he had a stash of loot, I'd go and spy on him with the other kids, sometimes he'd sit in front of his house for hours playing the flute with his big dog lying next to him, we were scared to get close, he must have known we were there but he didn't show it, some people in the village said he knew how to cast spells and tried to stay away from him, they even said he must be in cahoots with the devil and that the priest ought to go look around over there, only I think the priest was scared himself and in any case he turned a deaf ear, although in his case that wasn't too hard, you see, since he was actually a little hard of hearing, which complicated or simplified confessions, depending on how you look at it, because some people want the priest to really listen to them, and others prefer to just go psspsspss and receive their absolution, he had a huge stomach that bulged out under his cassock, and when he crossed his hands on top of all that like he was anchoring the edifice, you always worried he might blunder and tip, causing a general forwards collapse, you had to wonder how that man fit into the confessional, he must have felt like a canned sardine and it was quite a show to watch him work his way in there, he went in backwards, shifting his way one little jerk at a time, first to the right, then to the left, once he got his bottom firmly wedged in he'd pull the purple curtain across and wait for the first patient to kneel down and open the wooden screen on the side, at face-height and they'd get the cleansing underway, I wonder what people got out of coming to tell all their little stories, personally when I went I'd always embellish a little, sometimes I'd invent things outright, because if you're just going to tell the naked truth it's hardly worth going and smelling that guy's breath, I don't know exactly why, perhaps it was because of his weight, and I feel like saying his barrel, but when I think of that priest I always see him standing in front of a big mirror where he doesn't quite fit, I admit it's kind of silly, that all I'd have to do is make him move back a couple of steps so he wouldn't flow out onto the wall, so his whole body would fit in the mirror, but I just can't, you see, the image seems to be frozen forever in my imagination, the funniest thing was the day of the horse procession, they still did that back then, on a Sunday afternoon after the harvest and before they plowed the fields, the priest would go bless the fields so they would be fertile the following year, all the farmers in the area were there wearing their best clothes and riding their best horses, they'd bring a calm steed for the priest and hoist him up with the holy water and the sacrament, it was one of the biggest holidays of the year, people would make mountains of pies at home, and the kids would wander around stuffing their faces, you had to get a view of the priest at the head of the parade, all the farmers followed along single-file with flags and banners, he'd wear himself out trying not to fall and I can tell you one thing, it was a long jaunt, he had to bless every farmer's field, even the non-believers', the blues as we called them, there's always the worry of having an evil spell on the harvest, so better get your land blessed like everyone else, so the whole village was in on it and it took the priest all afternoon, lurching along on his nag and wielding his holy-water sprinkler, and every year he'd go through the same stations of the cross, one year a violent storm started just when the procession was furthest away from the village, you could see them out there on a dirt road in the middle of the fields, there was a dreadful rainstorm, with hail and lashing downpours and when they got back to the village it was like the retreat from Russia, the priest had even had to eat the ravaged holy sacrament because it was getting swept away in the flood, and as for the holy water it got extremely diluted, so as you can imagine, that poor priest, God rest his bones and ashes, he couldn't stand horses, his nightmares were full of long, galloping flights, falls and bruises, personally I've always felt a strange relationship between my dreams and real life, often when I was in a bad situation I've told myself it was only a dream and I could wake up, that I could just pinch myself to get out of the fix I was in, so I'd pinch myself but I was really surprised that it didn't wake me up, I'd try again more vigorously but forget it, it was still the same mess and although I'd closed my eyes when I'd pinched myself, the surroundings hadn't changed a bit when I opened them again, the strangest thing was that sometimes when I was sleeping and having a real nightmare, I'd end up dreaming I was pinching myself at the same time, it hurt but it wasn't enough to wake me up and my voyage through hell continued, finally when the morning came and pulled me out of dreamland it was awful, I had that journey stuck in my head, my mom kept telling me all day I was impossible and she'd never seen such a moody child, that I'd say white and change it to black five minutes later, but in fact I wished I could have been on the moon or anyplace a million miles away, as long as it wasn't with this wretched demon that had been after me all night and was still stealthily gnawing away at me, no chance of paying attention to anything, I went through that day like a sleepwalker, I was caught in the nightmare, it's like when you imagine you're only living as a character in someone else's dream, and there's always that fear that they'll wake up and everything will collapse, you're nothing but a puppet, a defenseless little pigeon waiting to be plucked, my buddy's favorite kind of pigeons were ladies of a certain age, but whose accounts were in order, with his gift of the gab he was a past master at this type of operation, he'd switch on the gallantry, offer to carry the lady's bags, he'd ask her if she had far to go and walk a little way with her, a touch of chit-chat, some wooing, one thing led to another and it was in the bag, he knew how to play on powerful emotions, you see, the lady would invariably remind him of a young girl he had loved, who'd died of tuberculosis, the difference, obviously, was that the girl didn't have a strong constitution, whereas the lady seemed to be blooming with health, in fact he'd noticed her right away because of her beautiful complexion, and so on ad infinitum because he could reel off that charming patter the way some people say their rosary, the upshot was a week or ten days' honeymoon to get the key to the moneybox, because the lady always wanted to express her gratitude after the hanky-panky, my buddy'd show up with a brand spanking new suit and ultra high-fashion Italian shoes, plus a few other little presents to brighten up the monotony of the weeks to come, after that, it was just a question of reversing the process and there'd be a great big scene of the other type, you see, he'd tell me, you can't let things go on too long, but he made it a point of honor to play by the rules, to finish the adventure with as much panache as he'd shown at the beginning, that guy was an artist, you see, so he'd explain to the lady that it was because he loved her that he wanted to leave her, they couldn't let something that had been so beautiful deteriorate, it was better to keep the incredible memory of that idyll, it had been the most intense experience of his life and never again would he feel such deep, sweet happiness, and although their paths were separating, she shouldn't cry, he said all this with great tact and all the necessary forms, in fact he explained to me that at a certain age women need these fleeting passions, it rejuvenates them, brings them back to life, and with that in mind it was only reasonable to expect them to loosen the purse strings a little, basically he'd made up a whole philosophy around the question and I even think it gave him a sense of social purpose to earn his living that way, the only thing that bugged him was occasionally there'd be a husband looking to cause him serious problems, especially if the lady hadn't held back when she'd opened the moneybags in gratitude, but it was pretty rare, because people generally don't want to get the police or their neighbors involved in that quintessentially private kind of situation, if you want to keep your reputation up, it's better to wash your dirty linen inside the family circle, work things out face to face, and often that cleaning would restore happiness to the home, there'd be a whole celebration on the theme of forgiveness, sensuous reunions, in short, the job suited my buddy to a T and allowed him to take long vacations living in mansions, I always liked it when he'd tell about his hanky-panky sessions, they were always full of froufrou and swooning, one day he found himself with a lady with a big canopy bed with white curtains all around it, they'd spent three days in there without coming out and you should have heard the story of that visit, the two of them had felt like Adam and Eve, they'd gone back to the most primitive wellsprings of love, rediscovered the instinctive animalistic rutting that man had long ago allowed to die, then as usual my buddy had abounded with digressions and comparisons, set the world right, in his own way, and I'm pretty sure it took all night, but when he was talking I had no sense of time passing, I was too absorbed by the continuous string of sentences, and he was getting more and more excited, his eyes were gleaming and he was gesticulating the whole time, it was as if his speech became the center of the universe, the stars were shining just to hear him better, the wind was humming along softly, and I was there with my mouth hanging open, everything he said fascinated me so much I felt I was sort of inventing it along with him, because you see his great power came from the way he made sure I felt involved with everything he said, as if without meaning to, almost naturally, I was providing half of the letters in his alphabet, although I didn't say anything, I was only listening, but my horse would swerve along with his, we'd take the steepest, soggiest paths, we'd go everywhere, we were kings and gods, and now that I'm here leading my steed alone, trying to cut the turns through all these memories, it's as if his voice were there supporting me, helping me make my way through the difficult sections, guiding me to places I wouldn't dare go alone, because whatever people say, there are some things that are hard to tell, you hesitate, procrastinate, you know, there are stories you wouldn't even share with your best friend, stories you try to bury once and for all in the most unobtrusive corner of your little imaginary garden, and if by some unfortunate chance they resurface one day, you feel so nauseous you'd rather be dead, all your limbs quiver, there was a guy who came here to be a farmer in the village, everybody liked him and then one day they found him hanged in his attic, they looked for a letter or a clue but he hadn't left anything, the only thing the police ended up finding out was that he was using a fake name, he took everything else to his grave, who knows what it was, what he had to drag around on his conscience for years until he couldn't take it anymore, in any case that story caused a huge stir around here, just like when it came out that Marie-Ange was having an affair with the stationmaster, she'd been working there at the station for a few months, she sold tickets at the window, and she's not even eighteen, said my mom indignantly, and that man has a wife and two kids, I must say it takes a real bitch to go chasing after an honest family man, basically that story was the only thing anyone talked about, there was quite a buzz and turmoil but don't worry, it all ended well, the sinner stopped working there overnight, her parents even kept her quarantined in her room for three or four weeks so she could think about the harm she'd done, and the stationmaster went on leave, he took a vacation to rest his mind and glands unless that was the time he had to go on a training program at a big station, I can't remember exactly, my mom also said the wife kept her dignity through the whole thing, she was a tall, skinny woman with her hair cut really short, at church on Sunday she kept a stern watch over her offspring and I imagined her at home with her dignity, sitting very stiffly in her chair and looking stoically at the wall in front of her, she didn't say anything, she didn't move, she kept her dignity through unhappiness, and incidentally, dignity in unhappiness was an expression I heard a lot, in my mom's mind that encapsulated the heroism of the betrayed woman who knew how to accept misfortune without grumbling, maintaining her stature, and there was no shortage of betrayed women in the area, it's like the wife of the justice of the peace who they found at the Tabarin when it burned down, the Tabarin was a bar with waitresses who took care of their customers on the main road going out of the village, it had a certain reputation and people came there from the city and even further away, then one night a girl was killed there, the fire demolished half of the building and apparently the judge had fallen asleep after his romp with a waitress, so he didn't wake up despite all the commotion from what was going on, he would have roasted alive if the flames had reached the room where he was sleeping, the police were the ones who shook him out of his dreams, umm, er, sorry to disturb you, Your Honor, but, you can imagine the scene, and since there were witnesses it was difficult to cover up the unlikely presence of that dignitary in a house of sin, that's why later on when they arrested the guy who killed the waitress the trial was held in-camera, sometime after that the judge moved away with his family and then his wife was able to keep showing her dignity someplace else, well, it might just be because of all that dignity they kept hammering into me, but I've always mistrusted people who can stay unflappable, who keep the same stony gaze in every situation, or people who can't cry, real sobbing, I mean, when your whole body's involved, with real shudders, it's completely different from that little tear at the corner of the eye, the type that makes such a good impression at weddings and funerals, my buddy loved to start a story with some colorful phrase that he'd suddenly drop, it was like his starting-point or take-off strip, you see, he'd say, then he'd stop for a minute, looking right into my eyes, and when he could see I was ripe, he'd trot out his little expression, crocodile tears, he'd yell, for example, and it seemed to me then that the whole story that followed would be just a way of il-lustrating those crocodile tears, showing them off, making them shine like a thousand candles, and they became more beautiful and precious than crystal, and whoever had cried them was filled with joy, as for the crocodile himself, you had the sense all through the story that he would have liked to be mentioned more often, he kept showing up at the slightest provocation, the animal I've always been afraid of is geese, the first few years when I was going to school they terrorized me every morning, once I got out of the big garden around the house I had to skirt the cemetery wall and then the road passed by two little farms about a hundred yards apart, both of these farms had a flock of geese, and those filthy creatures stayed close to the road all day, they could definitely tell I was dead terrified of them, I'd walk along furtively, I knew they were watching for me and my heart beat like one of King Michael's drums, I could often get past the first farm before they blocked my way, but the worst thing was when I got caught between fire from both sides, when the geese from the first farm had seen me and given chase and then the second flock appeared straight ahead, I still dream about those beasts, so when I'm talking about a woman and say she's a goose, let me tell you, coming from me the expression carries its own special charge of hate and spite, it's not just some banal and thoughtless comparison and I know what it means to talk, one day Marie-Ange's attitude to me changed, she started acting a lot nicer when we'd meet, she'd smile at me, we'd chat a little and soon things got more serious, or more frivolous, depending on your point of view, after all that time itching for it you can imagine the fiesta, I wanted her, I couldn't get enough and as soon as I saw her coming in her tight dress and with her long hair I'd start shaking, it was like flames rushing through my whole body, yes, it was summer and we'd hide in the wheat, my mom would say we saw you again with that tart, that worthless girl, you should be ashamed of yourself, and by the way you'll feel pretty smart when you come home with some disease, because that's what always happens with girls like that, a quick tumble in the ditch, but don't think you can expect me to feel sorry for you, you'll get just what you deserve, and she'd have a terrible fit, she'd be screaming all through the house and I'd usually just try to get out, it's true Marie-Ange had a bad reputation, she'd had a brush with all the whiskers around, you know, artichoke heart, a leaf for everybody, so all the women hated her, they would have killed her if they could, she's a maneater, they'd say, nobody else can wreck a home the way she does, I liked Marie-Ange a lot, pretty soon there was more to our relationship than hanky-panky, she'd tell me about her romantic adventures, her scores, I was her confidant and a lot of times she made me laugh with her boyfriend trouble, she always had two or three going at once, she'd lose track of her own head, and her legs too, and she'd tell me about it so candidly you would have handed her the holy infant without a confession, for her, men were just a question of appetite, if she was hungry she ate, she didn't see what the problem was, she'd even felt attracted to Victor, the old shepherd who lived alone in the middle of the fields, I always wondered what she saw in that guy, but people's taste is like colors, live and let live, I think despite his odd ways she found him handsome, and when you come down to it it's true he had a certain something, he was tall and thin with a long grey beard, when he came to the village he always wore a long black cape and a huge hat that made him look like someone from another age, he seemed to emanate some mysterious power, that's why people were frightened of him, and also people who are too quiet aren't normally very popular, people think they're not very frank, that they've got something to hide, so Marie-Ange started hovering around Victor, she'd find reasons to walk by his house, stop and have a little conversation, I don't know if she managed to get the shepherd's tongue working but in any case the charm took effect pretty quickly and it didn't take long before she added him to her list of conquests, he'd bring her into his little house and put the dog out, he probably didn't want the dog to see them romping, the weirdest thing was the way Marie-Ange, who told me about all her flings in full detail, and believe me when I tell you she wasn't scared of calling a spade a spade, she never said a word about her intimate affair with Victor, I tried to raise the topic several times but she just looked away, wouldn't answer or changed the subject and I quickly realized it wouldn't do any good to push her, then one fine day, I think it was a few months later if I remember correctly, they found Victor had been killed in front of his house, lying on his back, with coagulated blood covering a huge cut in his forehead, a little ways away they found the body of his dog, whose stomach had been cut open with a knife, probably when it was trying to defend its master and jumped at the attacker, was it someone who'd been tempted by the loot that Victor might have kept hidden in his house, it's possible, but in any case they never found out exactly what happened because they never caught the killer, and you can be sure it wasn't anyone from around here, Victor, see, he may have been weird, people respected him and they said in the village whoever did that couldn't take it with them to the afterlife, the police hunted around everywhere, they questioned everyone in the surrounding area but got nowhere, not the slightest clue, I remember it rained the day of the funeral, they buried the body in a completely untouched corner of the cemetery, when I was a kid I was fascinated by the will-o'-the-wisps, I'd see them sometimes when I was coming home in the evening in winter,it was pretty rare because they played hard to get, despite the cold I stayed for a really long time near the cemetery wall, I'd wait patiently for a little flame to suddenly come crackling to life in the darkness, and if by chance it happened I was filled with unbelievably intense joy, I felt so light, it was a sign for my benefit, ushering me into the realm of the night, making it hospitable, people in the village were scared of the will-o'-the-wisps, when I said I'd seen some, they'd cross themselves or say you shouldn't go looking around the tombs when you pass by there at night, it's true I've always had an inclination for some pretty macabre things, for example we had loads of fun sculpting beets, we'd take a nice, fat beet, carve the face of a particularly unappetizing old stiff into it with a knife, enhance the sculpture with some candle wax and then carve out the beet and stick the candle inside, and in the evening when everything was quiet, we'd go through the village streets and ring the bell where some woman lived alone, light the candle and when the woman opened the door, we were standing off to the side, in the dark, and we'd suddenly stick the beet in front of her face, you should have heard her scream, but one time there was a woman who unleashed her dog, the bitch, it was a German shepherd and we hadn't even run twenty yards before he got us, and of course I was the one who went down, he sank his teeth into my leg and pulled me down, and it was a good thing the old lady was there and called him off or I probably would have been dead, that mangy dog had me by the throat, I was moaning from the pain in my leg, which was bleeding loads, I thought it was broken because it hurt so much and the old lady was scolding me, in any case you deserved it, she concluded, and next time I'm calling the police, well I can tell you right now there was no next time, because I lost my taste for that type of game for a while, I went limping off into the night but the next day it was so infected I couldn't walk, we had to call the doctor, so I couldn't get out of telling my parents the truth, anyway the old lady had come over and told them in the morning, the sermons came on stronger than ever, you're just a good-for-nothing, a gangster in the making, you don't think of your poor dad who works from morning till night to feed you, you'll be the death of us with all your foolishness and spite, and la di da di da, my ears couldn't take any more, especially since I had to stay at home without moving my leg for several days, all I wanted to do was pack my stuff and clear off forever, see you later folks, I was thinking I could go sign up as a ship's boy, they'd never see me again and they better not expect a single postcard, but my leg healed and I didn't leave, that's how it always goes in the end, and also I wasn't more than nine or ten at the time and you forget quickly at that age, your head's like a weathervane and it's much better that way, it's crazy the number of things I heard that went straight in one ear and out the other, my mind's just like a sieve, and my memory's even worse, but the surprising thing is how the more I tell my little life story, the more memories rise to the surface, it's like vegetables in late summer, popping up all over the place, if it keeps going like that I'm going to get confused because it will be too much, but I realize I need to make an effort to organize all this, here I am galloping through my past in every direction and pretty soon you won't make out head or tail of it, I was just a little kid when my dad gave me a big red top, when it was spinning it made a shrill whistling sound, it sounded like an alarm siren and I could play with that thing for hours, the amazing thing is you can never tell which way the top will go, it just turns like crazy, it doesn't follow any law, see, it's just a blind machine that follows its secret instincts, this top had strange yellow pictures on it and when it was spinning, the drawings turned into a big solid line that would grow wider or thinner depending on the speed, then came the moment when the top started to get twitchy on its point, you could tell the final tumble was coming and the siren got deeper, gloomy even, I could catch it and set it spinning again before it tumbled, but if I did, I always waited until the very last second, I let it go right up to the brink of disaster, and the last second is the most marvelous, it's like when you're out at dusk, night falls and you keep watching the landscape, in a little while you think you can still see but actually for a while already you haven't been able to see a thing, you've gone over to the other side without realizing and all you're doing there is imagining the landscape, it's totally different, once I saw this film where some gangsters want to kill another gangster from a rival gang, they go out at night and put a big mirror in the middle of the road and the guy comes along at top speed in his sports car, he sees headlights hurtling straight towards him, he swerves hard trying to avoid them and goes smashing into the side of the road, it was pretty impressive because the side of the road was actually just a dead drop off a huge cliff into the sea, and even though it was at night, the film showed the skid and the plunge really clearly, they'd even had to hire a famous stunt man to pull it off, films are my passion, you know, I always shiver when the lights go down, when the film is about to start any second, everyone's sitting there like little kids, ready to embark on an amazing story, it's the moment when anything is possible, a religious moment, you're going to believe everything and at least there's no danger, because in real life you've got to always keep your guard up, there are always people ready to take you for a pigeon and pluck you clean, you always have to be wary of what people tell you, I can't stand it when people laugh at me, my buddy couldn't stand it either, although he knew how to look out for himself, you weren't going to get anywhere trying to fleece him if you weren't cagey, he worked as a street peddler in town for quite a while, they'd set him up with a counter on the sidewalk, in front of a big store, he was supposed to do a spiel for this so-called new type of device for cutting up vegetables more quickly, a joke, basically, but you couldn't imagine how successful he was, it was crazy, people would come pushing in on all sides to listen to him, the crowd would be spilling off the sidewalk, cars couldn't get by and during his working hours they'd had to post a policeman there permanently to direct traffic, and his words kept coming even faster than his vegetables, a fantastic and revolutionary device, ladies and gentlemen, at your service to get everything ready in one flick, two shakes of a soup spoon, three little stirs, fries, purées, salads, turnips, carrots, and off he went, it was like he'd found his calling, here I'll cut you up a leek and spice it up with three savory phrases, what's your name, young lady, lovely girl, Juliette, so here's Juliette's soup recipe, ladies and gentlemen, take an onion and slice it up fine, with our revolutionary tool it'll be done before you can even say you're going to do it, from now on your Sunday soup will be ready in a jiffy and you'll have the whole rest of the morning for hanky-panky, ah, what I wouldn't give to be your husband, Juliette darling, and he gave her this velvety glance that made everybody burst out laughing, he was selling his tools by the hundreds, in just a couple of days he must have become his bosses' goose with the golden eggs, but then one time he must have cut his onion a little too quickly or else he couldn't take his eyes off his Juliette that day, that's the technique, you see, you have to individualize the clientele, speak to each one in the singular, get a dialogue going from the start, so that revolutionary tool cut his finger to the bone, there was blood spurting all over his vegetables and he grimaced so badly people started to giggle, which he took really badly and then started shouting insults at them louder and louder, you bunch of poor halfwits, he was yelling, you're all hanging around like pigeons just waiting to be plucked, I mean you'd buy shorts buttons if you heard they were gold pieces, you think this tool's worth a red cent, in two days it's broken, I'm telling you, you can stick it in the garbage, trust me, and he was getting more and more excited and yelling at the top of his lungs, but the people who'd just bought one weren't thrilled to hear him trashing this thing they'd lusted after, they wanted their money back and started yelling, too, so that within a few seconds he was facing an angry mob while he was still holding his finger, which was bleeding profusely, the people in the front row were so furious, they knocked over the table with all the vegetables and kitchen tools, others were shaking their fists at him, they were getting more and more threatening, so he gave the guy closest to him a kick in the crotch, the funniest thing was he was still holding his cut finger with his other hand, then he got a punch in the face and somebody knocked him down, after that he got a proper thrashing, because there were a few of them all hitting him at once, and then the police finally pulled him out of there, but the experience left him extremely disillusioned, you see, he told me the next day, he had a black eye and a split lip, and he had a huge bandage around his hand, you see, that gig's a job for losers, no way am I doing that again, they can find someone else to flog their damn junk, you see my buddy couldn't stand to fail, it drove him completely wild, there was this boy at school who always worked till he dropped, but he had to be number one, he put all his strength and rage into it, when he looked at us his eyes were full of hate, he saw us as rivals who could always be a threat, even though most of us didn't have anything like that kind of ambition, me, for example, I didn't

care that much about being top in the class but that was all he
thought about and he was top student for years, then once, by some
unfortunate chance, someone finished the year with a higher grade
than he did and he was really embarrassed, he would have liked to go
apologize to Cram, that was his name, or the nickname we'd given
him, and tell him he hadn't done it on purpose, but the look on
Cram's face was dreadful, he was dripping with anger and humilia-
tion, the principal came to hand out the report cards and he was
flabbergasted, so, Cram, what happened, he asked, and Cram turned
bright red and didn't answer, it's like Caesar, first in the village rather
than second in Rome, the teacher had told us that story admiringly
but everyone was looking at Cram and giggling, the poor guy didn't
know where to squirm, his eyes were flashing even deadlier machine-
gun fire than usual, then one day, it must have been a few months
later, we'd had more than enough of Cram and decided we were going to settle his score once and for all, we'd form a court and he'd be
judged, we went and found him during recess, made him sit down
and sat in a circle around him, there was a deathly silence hanging
over the schoolyard, Cram was looking at the ground and didn't dare
move, somebody stood up and went over to him, and now Cram, he
said, you're going to explain why you never speak to anyone, why
you hate everybody, right then the teacher came running up, he'd
been watching what was going on for a while and must've been getting increasingly worried, what are you little rascals up to, I order
you to leave this poor boy alone, and he was so worked up he started
kicking in every direction to make us clear off, then he took Cram by
the arm, helped him up, and brought him back to the classroom,
apparently Cram's parents came to see the principal that evening and
the next day we found out he was transferring to a school in town,
and good riddance, although at first being back in class without
Cram felt really weird, it felt kind of like when they cut down a tree
in front of your window or you have a tooth removed, it takes a
while to get used to it, and also we felt guilty in the end, because the
teacher had given us an interminable sermon on our cruelty, and

actually, if he hadn't come over to save Cram I'm really not sure how things would have played out, those kinds of situations often finish pretty badly, it wasn't just some game, in any case it can be tricky to make a distinction between what's a game and what's serious, it's like those people you meet sometimes who actually say much more when they're joking than when they talk sternly, it's that old story about the book and its cover, just look at Marie-Ange with her reputation, everybody said it's in that girl's blood, she'll never change, but you know she still became my girlfriend, well and truly, and loyal, and also I wonder if maybe I exaggerated about her a little, it's true she'd had a handful of affairs, but after all, sometimes you've got to try on a lot of shoes before you find one that fits, Marie-Ange was the one great love of my life, in comparison to what I experienced with her the rest doesn't even matter, it's like wind, just for the pleasure of the hanky-panky, and the girls could tell, too, they'd often say you're in love with somebody else, or they'd say you've been deeply in love in the past, I can tell, what's her name, because you know how passion leads you by the nose once it wraps its golden arms around you, and it's true I'm a hopeless romantic, but you wouldn't believe how often I've told myself the story of the life we'd lead together, Marie-Ange and I, the children we'd have, and even how we'd die together romantically, hand in hand, she was beautiful, with big green eyes that took up most of her face, her hips swayed a bit when she walked and all the boys would turn to watch as she passed by, I was really proud of that, and with her I had the feeling that everything I did had a purpose, my life was no longer one long gallop with no goal, all hodge-podge, and deep down I always wanted someone settled, with a really organized life, a little like those beautiful, well-maintained gardens with wide gravel paths to walk on, flower beds for getting sentimental and thickets for hanky-panky and then hidden some-place in the back wall, behind the gardener's shed, a big junk-hole for discreetly dumping the body, I always thought it sounded funny when people talked about having a body on their hands, near our house there was this well called dead-man's well and I'll let you guess why the water wasn't drinkable anymore, Emile, honey, where are we going to stick my husband now that we've slain him, there was also a place I really liked, which was the spot where they'd leave the compost to decompose, they'd put a huge heap of leaves there to rot and it made a rich, black, pungent compost, there were hundreds of earthworms living in there, which the fishermen loved, my buddy hated fishermen because they can't stand people making noise around them, you can't talk to them, and the one thing he always needed was an audience, although actually most people liked him around here, they thought he was a character and when he was little he must have swallowed some kind of talk motor with a great big propeller, but once he started firing off phrases over the mountains, everybody would listen, I think his style of word theater gave people a little dose of dream-life, his speeches were like those endless freight trains, there you are at the railway crossing counting the train cars going by and even when they're gone there are more of them, you start to wonder where they get trains strong enough to pull all that, and my buddy did voices, he'd go from deep ones to high ones, from harsh ones to melodious ones with the skill of a conjurer, and just when you least expected it, right at the most thrilling part of the story, he'd suddenly stop as if he'd forgotten the rest, you should have heard the silence at that moment, nobody dared to breathe, they were anxiously hoping he'd remember how the story went, and when it came to him and he got started again, the audience gave a sigh of relief, I should tell you how we became inseparable friends, it was because of a glove, just a regular wool glove, when I was going to school in winter I was always losing my gloves and some winters my mom had to buy me four or five pairs in a matter of weeks, so every morning before I left I'd get inspected, let me see your gloves, and when I'd lose one I'd spend the whole evening thinking about the terrible, fateful moment I had to look forward to the next morning, with the whole big scene and the slap I'd get, I was hoping for a miracle, the house could burn down, for example, the thing with the gloves became an obsession, you know, in fact that's probably why I lost them so often, in the evening

I kept turning over and over in bed and then came the dreadful awakening, when I left the peace of my dreams and landed in that cruel morning when I'd have only one glove to show, I'd have to admit I had lost the other one, I wished so badly I could pinch myself and get back to dreamland, I bathed and got dressed like a robot, my heart beating as I saw it coming quicker and quicker, the awful point when my mom would say it's time to leave, that I needed to get my coat on, I was praying to every saint in heaven to send me a small miracle at the last second, any kind of miracle, some uncle from Australia could suddenly come ring the doorbell, or some news, war, flood, any epidemic you like as long it made her forget I was supposed to show her those miserable pieces of wool, it was a long way to school in the cold, and still, I would have gladly agreed to go gloveless for the whole winter, but no, it was a key principle of my upbringing, I had to learn to keep track of my things and it had crystallized into those godforsaken gloves, I can still hear her voice, show me your gloves, so I'd slowly pull out the one I had left, that spared me a couple of seconds, then I started searching for the other one, I reached into the very bottom of my pockets, I dug around and pulled out a bunch of very interesting items but no dice, no second glove, I made a surprised, slightly stupid face, she looked steadily at me and waited, without saying a word, I put on a tiny voice, it's really strange, I can't find it, I'm sure it was there, then she started to yell, frighteningly loudly, don't you tell me you've lost another glove, I've never been so ashamed in my life as at those times, I wished the ceiling could fall on our heads and kill us both, and when I felt the slap it was almost like a release, that meant the nightmarish moment between admitting my wrong and receiving the sentence was finally over, the moment that seemed to take centuries, when I could have just crawled down into the earth, the moment when time was frozen, inhuman somehow, now I could open the door, set off on the walk to school, even if I was crying, even if I had to wear a cowl of infinite sadness the whole way, the point of death was behind me, yes, that's what I used to call that tortured instant, then one time the miracle happened,

I was on my way back from school and came into view of the house when I realized I only had one glove, we'd had a snowball fight and I'd stuffed my soaked gloves into my pocket, a lot of times that was how disaster struck, and now it had struck again, I retraced my steps to the area where the snowball fight had been, looking everywhere, but no glove in the snow any more than in my pocket, plus it was almost dark already, it was totally unfair, the whole world was against me, you know, it hadn't even been three days since the last glove I'd lost, so it was really bad timing, I didn't even want to think about the particularly awful scene this would cause and I won't tell you how I spent that night, but in the morning, only a minute or two before the culmination of the tragedy, suddenly, someone rang the bell, I ran to the door, it wasn't the uncle from Australia, it was my buddy's friendly face and guess what that guy was holding in his hand, he must have thought I was nuts because I jumped up and hugged him, but it was as if he'd saved my life, from then on we became the world's best friends, he'd also been in the snowball fight the day before, and this time he'd stayed longer than I did and picked up my glove lying out on the battlefield, it's incredibly important to have good friends, friends who you can tell anything, who understand you, who sup-port you through hard times, it's like when my parents were yelling that I was just putting on airs, a fine lot of good it had done trying to get me to study, and it was time I learned a trade, Marie-Ange was always there telling me not to listen to them, do as you see fit and if you don't feel like working don't work, just getting your hands dirty won't necessarily make you happy, after all you're only young once and you've got to make the most of it, that was when I usually spent the day drawing with charcoal, and although I don't want to brag I'll admit I was always pretty good at drawing, of course these days I'm out of practice, but at the time nobody could beat me at sketching a landscape or conveying atmosphere, Marie-Ange loved posing for me and I drew her meticulously from every angle, plus it put us both in the mood for hanky-panky, we were lusty little scamps, we'd kiss for hours till we had no mouths left and stay in the saddle forever, in long, unbridled sessions that left us drunk with happiness and fatigue, sometimes I also did caricatures, there was one I did of my buddy that I kept for a long time, I drew him with a gigantic mouth and teeth that looked ready to devour everything in reach, I'm not sure if it's because he was chatty, but he had a huge appetite, he could gobble up one plate after another, and he'd eat the last one as quickly as the first, and you should have seen the heap of potatoes he'd serve himself from the pot, once he started wolfing it down he hardly knew anyone else was there, and I've seen him eat like that for almost an hour without pausing, his face turned red and he looked so involved you would have thought that was the most important part of his existence, the thing is, he'd tell me, eating is the number one fundamental activity, there's no funny business with food, it goes straight to your body, I'm hungry, I fill it, fill it up as much as needed, and my buddy was right, because there's nothing more pathetic than those people who eat half-heartedly, who hardly seem to touch their food, you'd think they're scared of life, trying to keep away from it, although you'll notice most people like that are cranky sourpusses, Marie-Ange had an honest appetite, she didn't whine about her diet and her figure, she'd say this is how I am and anybody who doesn't like it can go chase themselves, and being plump really suited her, she lived her life to the fullest and that's why she understood what I went through during my two months in prison, I was thinking about her day and night, she came to visiting hours one Sunday and when I saw her there sitting across from me with tears in her eyes, I realized how powerful our love was, we just looked at each other without saying a word the whole time until she left, we understood each other completely with no need to talk, and I could tell by her face she didn't blame me for any of it, she still trusted me completely, she knew the whole thing was an accident, that I was no thug, and she could see in my eyes I'd never do it again, that it was just a bad dream and once I woke up everything would go back to normal, anyway it had been my buddy's idea to steal the bag, that guy was tough, you know, and I'm pretty sure I was dying of fear, we'll get caught, I told him, it's too dangerous, but he waved off my

objections, this kind of thing's in the bag was how he put it, what do
you think's going to happen, only what did happen was I got nabbed
and he slipped away, I refused to give the police his name so they
beat me up, forget it, you'll never get anything out of me and anyway
I did it on my own, and that pissed them off even more since everyone had seen there were two of us, and also the old lady had said the
one who'd hit her had managed to clear off, but friendship was important to me, it really meant something, they could have killed me
and I wouldn't have talked, and later when we met up my buddy
thanked me, with feeling, he just said it's hard to find friends like you,
and shook my hand, I didn't brag, I said anyone would have done the
same thing, I never liked drawing attention to the good things I did,
I can't stand those so-called heroes you meet on every corner who are
always ready to tell you their most recent exploits, I'm the discreet
type, you know, there's no reason to make a mountain out of a mole-
hill, but some people think whenever they do something a little unusual it's like they've managed to make the earth spin backwards, and
you realize that'll happen once in their lives at most, because the rest
of the time they've got their tidy little lives, one drawer for work, one
drawer for the Sunday service, one drawer for love, and when it comes
to hanky-panky, let's not lose our cool, nothing there to fuss about,
don't forget married couples need to respect each other whatever
happens, I had a grandmother whose nightshirts came down to her
ankles, extremely respectable clothing, but there was a slit right where
you'd guess and a very pious inscription all around the slit, if it be
God's will or something like that, but you can bet the bucks had a
field day at the Tabarin, they'd make up for lost time, it was the
safety valve, only it had to stay out of view, in the shadiest part of the
garden, me, I prefer people who aren't afraid to let their true colors
show, take Victor for example, that man couldn't care less what people said about him, he lived as he pleased, period, I think I told you
there were people who didn't like him, but what I haven't told you is
some people didn't mind his company, and they were all of the fe-
male sex, because old Victor was what you call a horn-dog, the guy

was really into his hanky-panky, sure, he lived alone in the middle of the fields but I'll tell you, he had plenty of visitors, and it was a different lady visiting every time, he had a big dog, a German shepherd if I remember right, and when he was busy fornicating he'd put his dog outside, it even turned into a kind of signal, if we were walking by and saw the dog by itself in front of the house, we knew for sure his master was off frolicking on cloud nine with one of his lovely ladies, Victor was a real billy-goat, when you saw how ugly he was you'd wonder what they saw in him, actually it might have been to do with some woman that he got killed, some jealous husband or jilted lover, who knows, but he could have at least tied his dog up when he'd leave it out on its own, that was one dangerous animal and one day it attacked my buddy who happened to be prowling in the area, it bit him so badly he had to stay at home for weeks and he was walking with crutches for a long time after that, old Victor hardly even apologized, you often hear that country people are crude, which isn't always true, although it was different from the city and I have to admit the city atmosphere intimidated me a bit, one time my buddy took me to the city to visit one of his aunts, it was during vacation, we were supposed to stay over and come back the next day, my mother had dressed me up and offered a ton of advice, and my buddy explained that his family looked down on this aunt because of her bad luck, she'd married a strange guy who'd left her a few years later to become a sailor, but in any case, because she bore her misfortune with dignity, people felt bad for her in the end, me, I was wary of this dignified aunt, but my buddy said not to worry, I'd see she was really nice, and it's true this one wasn't at all like my idea of a very dignified aunt, she was pretty young, slender and tall, with long hair, which she wore loose, flowing down her back, that night, she took us out to eat, I'm so proud to go out with little gentlemen like you, she said, and the little gentlemen, who were maybe somewhere around thirteen or fourteen, tried to look the part in such a fancy place, his aunt talked about lots of interesting things and kept smiling at me, after that we went home and she showed us our rooms, we stayed up talking for a while and then went to bed, I was already asleep when someone shook me softly and there she was, looking at me, laughing, she was incredibly beautiful, wearing a transparent nightgown, you know, that was the first time something like that happened to me and I thought I was dreaming, she put her finger to my mouth so I'd know to keep quiet, then took my hand and I followed her to her room, there was a big canopy bed with white curtains all around, the aunt closed the door and came close to me, I could see her magnificent breasts through her nightgown and her lips touched mine, sometimes when I'm talking about something it's like a voice inside me interrupts, it says you're laying it on too thick, sucker, it's getting boring, give it a rest, I'm sure you know the kind of awkward situation I'm talking about, probably been through it yourself, where you're showing off, everyone does it, even the most modest people, and you suddenly realize there's someone in the audience who knows exactly what's going on, and could put you in your place with a single word, I remember one time my buddy started telling people he'd been a boxer and become regional champion, he got all the girls there to come feel his biceps, 'cause I don't know if told you already, but he was in pretty good shape, so what with his feats of boxing and uppercuts here and there, he even stood up to act out his role, gesturing and getting all worked up, so right then, he explained, I hit him dead on, he was hopping around with his guard up, so absorbed in the story and the live demonstration he didn't notice this one guy come in, sort of a cousin on his mother's side, and the guy was sitting there chuckling softly, 'cause, unfortunately for my buddy, the cousin had been boxing for a while, he was even about to go pro, then he started laughing louder and louder, and finally my buddy heard it, he suddenly turned to see which upstart would dare, but when he saw the upstart was his cousin, let me tell you, he went whiter than a corpse, the poor guy sure wasn't expecting a run-in like that, the cousin goes, well boy, emphasizing the boy part, you're so strong, how come we never see you down at the gym, and people started laughing, especially the girls, and I could see my buddy start dripping sweat, he stammered something nobody could understand, so the cousin suggested a friendly little match, to give the audience something to watch, instead of speeches, only my buddy had seen his cousin boxing a few times before, and he wasn't too keen to jump in, I watched him fall pitifully silent, he didn't even answer, just pretended to laugh with the others, then when he thought no one was looking, he slipped away discreetly, in the evening I found him completely drunk, he saw me and started crying, I was kind of touched, since I'd never seen him cry before, then he went off, I'll kill him, I'll kill him, he kept yelling, it was such a gripping spectacle, the waiter didn't dare interrupt the show to throw him out, even though my man was breaking glasses and the café was looking more and more like the St. Bartholomew's Day massacre, but all of a sudden he broke down and started crying again, he was holding his head in his hands and making little whimpering sounds, then he threw up and calmed down a little, I even had to help him get up and take a piss, and he ended up falling asleep, but you can imagine, he didn't want to hear a word about his cousin, you know, nobody wants to look like a braggart, a blowhard or a faker, although there are some brilliant fakers, just look at the guy who went to prison for painting Rubens and Velazquez, or whatever it was, anyway the paintings were truer than life, so after a while there were too many Rubens and Velazquez up for sale, maybe even two exactly the same sometimes, no way to tell which was real and which was fake, with fake bank notes they say there's always a slight difference, if you look closely at the top left corner you can see the tip of the ear is a little longer on the fake, sure, but still, everything else is exactly the sameand it takes some skill to make a copy like that, did you ever think how weird the expression controlled origin is, for wine, because half the time it's impossible to control anything at all, let's say you get the idea to check the authenticity of everything around you, well good luck, sooner you than me, and who knows, for example, if your friends' feelings for you are really what they seem, I mean, I should tell you one of the key episodes of my great passion for Marie-Ange, because that was love in its big, pure, glorious form, I would have given my life for Marie-Ange, I would have jumped in front of a train if I had to, so anyway, I can remember one time she got sick, it was serious, we thought she wouldn't make it and called the doctor in the middle of the night, and the thing was, it was winter, the roads were covered with snow, in fact it was still snowing, the doctor's car had to be dug out of the snow on the other side of the village, when he finally came to examine Marie-Ange, he realized she needed medication as soon as possible, but he didn't have the medication with him, someone had to go back to town for it and with the wind there were snowdrifts all over the roads, the doctor wouldn't have made it through by car, so I volunteered right away and took off on my motorcycle, it was a hell of a ride and it felt like I'd never arrive, my hands hurt so badly even with thick gloves that a few times I had to stop and try to warm them up as best I could, the cold went straight through me all over and you couldn't see six feet in front of you, and I kept having to get off the bike and walk it because the snow was too deep, but I had Marie-Ange's face flashing through my head, she was smiling at me and keeping me warm, I knew she was counting on me, that I was her only hope and nothing could stop me, and when I finally arrived at the town pharmacy I'm pretty sure I rang the bell like a maniac, enough to wake up the whole street, before I left with the precious medication the pharmacist gave me a big glass of spirits, I could see the admiration in his eyes for the feat I was accomplishing, but I didn't care about that, see, the only thing that mattered was saving Marie-Ange and the hero's medal could wait, the way back was even worse, my eyes were running with the blinding whiteness, I was dead with cold and fatigue and then on the way to the village I ran out of fuel, I had to leave the motorcycle and finish that awful trek on foot, I was in a world of pain, but what a thrill when they saw me arrive, the doctor gave her a shot right away, Marie-Ange was saved and the whole family thanked me, as soon as I could I went home quietly, in any case I was just doing my duty, and those experiences stay in your head, and the memories cheer you up when you need it, they're the ones you want to plant in the middle of the garden, and cherish them, water them every night, and spend your free time pulling up weeds around them, I wish I had a memory as sharp as my buddy's, he could remember everything, you'd think he had his whole life filed away in his head like the sheets in my mom's wardrobe, mine's more like the roads in Babylon,swarming, skulking in every cranny, just try to make sense of a jumble like that, every so often I wish I could replay a couple of days of my life, like in the movies, I mean not just any day because I wouldn't want to leave it to chance, there are some you'd rather forget, but one of those calm little days where you let time pass without realizing, one of these little grey days, all gentle and melancholy, because memories always come and go and disappear too soon, memory's a real vagabond, if you'll pardon the expression, and there goes another caravan of memories disappearing out into the desert, deep in the silver screen, as the sun sets and we see the end in big, red, slightly shimmering letters, that's memory's final scene, between life and the grave, and let's have a skeleton with all its bones bleached by the sun in the foreground, towards the left, the strange thing is I can't remember the features of the guy who attacked Marie-Ange, although I remember everything else that happened, I don't know why, that face just won't come out of the shadows, something inside me wants to keep it hidden, it was springtime and everything smelled good, you know that time of year that lasts only a few days, flowers start showing on all the trees, everything awakens, and suddenly, you find yourself wondering why you're out there, head in the clouds, wearing the big coat you wore all winter, it was getting dark and I was on my way home, I was just coming to the cemetery when I heard a scream in the field near there, my heart skipped a beat because I recognized Marie-Ange's voice, she was screaming help, help, I ran over there and saw them right away, they were in the middle of the field and the guy was dragging her by the arm, she was trying to resist, but I'll tell you, she was never that strong, he threw her on the ground and right then I came up and grabbed him from behind, he got a hell of a thrashing, didn't look pretty afterwards, I think one punch even broke a couple of his teeth, his right cheek swelled up and turned a lovely shade of brick red, and he was limping, then I told him to get lost, and we better not catch him prowling around again, and went over to Marie-Ange, who'd been watching the whole thing, shaking, I picked up her shawl,which was lyingon the ground, I shook off the dirt sticking to it and wrapped it around her shoulders, the guy had cleared off without further ado, I took Marie-Ange gently by the arm and led her back to the path, she was shivering, pressed up against me, we didn't say anything, we walked along slowly and little by little she regained her calm, although she was still kind of in shock for a couple of days, she needed plenty of peace and quiet to recover, she was like a convalescent, and I remember we went for a long walk in the fields, it was even the same day she told me she'd like to have children, and when you come down to it, that was a time when I was happy, living on love alone, not worried about a thing, sure, there are plenty of people with harder lives than mine, after all, I shouldn't start complaining now, and moaning about my luck, I may have had some rough times, like everyone else, but I also had happy times, and let me tell you, just the fact that I can tell you my little history, even if I'm telling it clumsily, still does me good, it gives me courage for whatever comes next in this life, I wish I'd lived back when people travelled from place to place telling stories, this way, my friends, right this way, and they'd beat the drum in the village square, come join in with our great burlesque theater, shed real tears listening to the story of our dreadful suffering, dream with our dreams, tremble with fear in our most horrible nightmares, come laugh at the tale of our most un- likely pranks, blend your lies with our truth and your truth with our lies, come one, come all, my buddy used to love Laurel and Hardy films and he'd roar with laughter when they hit each other in the face with a cream pie, he also noticed they had a special technique for that kind of scene, you see, he said, those guys go back and forth playing the pigeon for each other, every time one of them throws a pie, he gets into the best possible position to get creamed by the next one, they're such idiots they'll even help their opponent, Laurel's carrying a big box and Hardy grabs his chance to stamp on Laurel's foot, and Laurel grimaces with pain, but right afterwards he hands Hardy the box, as if to ask him to kindly hold it for a minute, and Hardy naively goes along with it, thinking he's being helpful, but it was obviously just a ploy to immobilize his arms, so he can't defend himself, because what does Laurel do as soon as Hardy takes the box, well, since he's got his hands free, he dips his finger into a can of white paint that just happens to be sitting on the table and draws what looks like Indian war paint on Hardy's face, at which point he considers his work with satisfaction, while Hardy discovers his new face in a mirror that happens to be passing by and doesn't seem too thrilled to be decorated like that, so he sets the big box on the table, takes the can of paint, and hands it to Laurel as if to ask him to kindly hold it for a minute, and this idiot Laurel naively takes it, when it's obviously just a ploy, because what does Hardy do once Laurel takes the can of paint, well, since he's got his hands free, he takes a paintbrush that's also on the table and dips it vigorously into the can, while Laurel watches him with curiosity and what even looks like interest, then Hardy starts painting white all over not only Laurel's face, but his neck, the top of his shirt, his tie and collar and the cuffs of his jacket, and when he's finished, he considers his work with satisfaction, while Laurel seems visibly not 100% pleased, and then since Laurel himself no longer has any reason to keep holding the can of paint, he puts it on the table, grabs the paintbrush from Hardy, and sets it next to the can, after which he takes Hardy's hat and asks him to hold it for a second, and even though at this point, it's hard to believe it could be just a simple favor, there goes Hardy, like the biggest pigeon of all, holding the hat for Laurel, who takes the can of paint and dumps its contents into the hat, and having set down the paint can, pulls the hat down onto Hardy's head, and so on, and my buddy, who'd been acting out the whole scene as he went along, was convulsing with laughter, I've got to say, he was a born actor, there was nobody like him for impersonations, he could do a perfect imitation of anybody's voice, they say some people can hear voices, like voices from beyond the grave, I get scared when I can't understand what's going on, you know like when reality becomes fiction, or viceversa, I forget which, when it becomes impossible to separate the wheat from the chaff, to accept people, flaws and all, you can sense a terrible threat without knowing where it's coming from, whether it's real or imaginary, don't laugh about it, sometimes it's as dangerous as the sword of Damocles, it could fall on you at the drop of a hat, it's like in the movies when the guy goes home, no worries, opens the closet and finds a body, and even though he doesn't recognize the dead person, you can imagine he could have done without that, just try explaining to the police that it's nobody you know, those people are suspicious, they're always sniffing in all the corners, no thanks, I've got no desire to be their pigeon, believe me, I'd rather just keep telling my little stories, cultivate my garden, as the philosopher said, one day someone called my buddy Caracala, I really can't remember why, but still, the name stuck, it reached the point where if someone was rambling on a bit, we'd say you're starting to sound like Caracala, you have to admit it's got a nice ring to it, Caracala, when I was little there were names that fascinated me, like Tartar, I'd imagine these cruel warriors riding little horses whose bellies touched the ground, they'd charge, saber aloft, howling, with splendid multicolored turbans on their heads, for a long time, I thought it was Tartarar instead of Tartar, and I was king of the Tartarars, we'd go raiding all over the place and end up conquering the whole world, nothing could withstand the strength and ferocity of my hordes, and my hero was this one knight, his name was Bohemond of Tarente, Bohemond accomplished the most amazing feats, got out of the most inextricable traps, he'd cut down hundreds of infidels on the battlefield, save people at death's door from the cruelest torture, widows and orphans, and all the horseback rides and campaigns we went through together, Bohemond and I, all the times I saved his life, or he saved mine, but one day an even more fabulous name entered my life, the illustrious name of Tartarin of Tarascon,

Tartarin was both an invincible warrior and irresistible seducer, I should tell you I came across his name at that age when you get curious about what happens behind the veil, and the slightest word that relates to hanky-panky makes you prick up your ears, so to speak, and as far as hanky-panky goes, Tartarin of Tarascon knew what he was doing, no kidding, so with Tartarin, I'd spend some time with the ladies, I had a great big canopy bed where I'd treat them to all the honors befitting them, I'd hardly get up long enough to settle scores with a few villains, save twenty-odd damsels in distress at the same time, then right back to hanky-panky, I even think towards the end I preferred staying in bed and sending good old Tartarin out to do battle alone, but one day I came across a book, and this book's title was the eminent name of my sidekick in seduction, you can imagine how curious I was, Tartarin of Tarascon wasn't just some name, the name had a story, I was about to go from my dreams to reality and find out who he was, my heart was pounding and I sat down with the book in a nice quiet corner, I reverently opened it, but after a few pages, what a disappointment, this Tartarin was nothing but a braggart, a trickster, a façade, nothing but a façade, a poor jerk trying to fleece everyone, and me believing him all these months, I'd brought him with me on the most heroic and lascivious conquests, it was a rude awakening, for sure, and the more I read, the more cold disgust I felt for this loser, I disowned him, I crossed his name off the list of humanity, he might as well have been dead to me, in fact I forgot him so completely it wasn't till now, I swear, so many years later, that his name came back to me, it might have been better to leave it buried, too, you never get anywhere spending your time chasing all these ghosts, it's no good dwelling on painful memories, and really, you can always find something upbeat, even in the saddest events, just take my time in prison, of course it wasn't much fun, but I could have been worse off, my cellmate liked to joke around and I had some good times with him despite everything else, he was in for a few-weeks, too, for some kind of smash and grab, as he told me when we met, the day I arrived, even the way he pronounced the words smash

and grab struck me favorably, smash and grab sounds somehow violent and jaunty at the same time, you know, joyful and meaty, it
sounds like a smooth, effortless entry, first you smash, then you grab,
and off you go, loot in hand, I don't know why but the phrase smash
and grab always reminds me of hanky-panky, this way, this way young
ladies, I'm king of the smash and grab, the bonny prince of velvet, we
have no truck with gloom around here, believe me, climb in my boat,
we're setting out for the isles, the blue isles, to tell the truth, life will
be like a dream, there are endless beaches, love potions, enchanting
perfumes, some people say you can control your dreams, in the evening before bed you place your order, tonight it'll be an Asian princess
with enormous eyes, I'd also like a beautiful bedroom with a huge
blue marble bath in the middle, sofas and cushions all around, a flute
orchestra, and then during the night bring a light repast, something
delicate, seafood, an exotic salad, honey cakes, a fruit platter, because
to tell you the truth I've got a thing about the Far East, I prefer ori-
ental palaces to castles in the air, I've always been fascinated with that
story where a princess told the sultan the next part of an ongoing
story every night, which she invented as she went, and she had good
incentive to use her imagination, since she knew she'd be put to death
if the sultan ever found her story boring, imagine Caracala in that
role, no problem for him, the sultan would have died of old age before the story finished, unless Caracala decided to make him die
laughing, because when he wanted his listeners rolling on the floor
laughing, he tickled them with a great big ostrich feather, that guy
was such a clown, nobody could resist once he got going, they could
hardly take it, they'd be writhing, laughing to tears, and he'd be steer-
ing the gondola, unruffled as anything, measuring his effects, calculating his angles the way a watchmaker precision-tightens the springs
of a watch, making everyone laugh like that might have been when
Caracala felt at the height of his powers, one time I tried to keep my
distance, to stick enough wax in my ears so I could hear just the
minimum, I mainly wanted to watch what happened, pay attention
to his game, he got people laughing, drawing them into a pretty

unlikely story, all I can remember was it involved some extremely drunk guy who the police picked up in a ditch, he had a cheerful tone, Caracala, and a quick flow with sudden changes of pitch, he used loads of funny expressions and people were laughing harder and harder, I mean after a few minutes pretty much everyone was laughing uncontrollably, I was over in my corner and I didn't take my eyes off my buddy, his face gradually transformed and pretty soon you could see a kind of satisfaction, here it came, he'd managed to get the crowd in his hand, the audience was at his mercy, he could do what he liked with them, and then his face started shining, he was relishing his power, enjoying the force he wielded, then suddenly you had the sense that he wanted to test the limits of that power and force, as if he liked taking some risks, and his flow did slow down imperceptibly, he was waiting a little longer between each sentence for the laughter to die down before whipping it up again, I had the impression that slowly but surely a kind of diffuse anxiety was creeping into the laughter, and that he, Caracala, was stirring that anxiety on purpose, people were definitely still laughing, but it was as if they could tell the person making them laugh so much was gradually dropping them, not stoking their enjoyment so insistently, there was even one fleeting moment when the audience's disappointment became clearer, right away he turned the voltage up all the way, he fired off a couple of quicker, more varied phrases and the contagious laughter started up all over again, even stronger, he was just toying with his power a little, he'd let things drift a little without reaching the point of no return, just brushing up against it, and his face right then took on a strange grimace, frozen, preoccupied, like the face of a kid pulling a beetle's legs off, I was scared, that's right, I felt really scared of that guy, because, see, all these amazing stories, all his fine talk, it was just a way to turn people into pigeons and pluck them, to lead them wherever he liked without their being able to do anything to defend themselves, and ever since then I've been wary of people who talk too well, there's a reason they say silver-tongued, whereas silence is golden, I like people who don't talk much but whose words you can tell are deliberate, carefullychosen, useful, these people don't talk for no reason, I like essential, definitive sentences, that's why I've always liked mottoes and proverbs, it's wonderful to be able to sum up the whole meaning of a life in two or three words, onwards and upwards, courage and fidelity, I will maintain, or all the popular wisdom that language carries with it, the straw that breaks the camel's back, counting your chickens before they're hatched, the priest had trouble talking, sometimes he almost stuttered and I have to say his Sunday sermons were pretty boring, in that area he didn't exactly follow in Caracala's footsteps, you'd listen patiently and twiddle your thumbs, watch the flies circling, count the candles under the statue of the Virgin, yes, I know, some people are going to say look who's talking, I've been boring them stiff for quite a few pages already, and they'd like to know what the point is, the village priest may not have been an orator but at least he wasn't just talking for no reason, come on people, let's not get carried away, it's easy to judge people superficially and if some people think I can't hold the reins on my story, I'd like to ask them to stay with me, later on they'll understand and say I was right, you know for a long time as child I was withdrawn and taciturn, I didn't have a lot of friends and I often got bored, for a year or two I was an altar boy with that guy Cara, it was more fun than just listening to the service doing nothing, and also for the big ceremonies we got to swing the censer, and there are few things more enjoyable than that, we were always arguing over who'd be in charge of that incredible gadget, finally we agreed to take turns, but every time it was the other person's turn, we'd use every dishonest trick in the book to claim it wasn't, that it was actually our turn and the arguments went on and on, you see, the censer's a device that requires constant attention, at least once the piece of coal that's used to burn the incense is lit, you have to keep swinging the thing all the time, keep it going from right to left and left to right to give the coal some air and keep it burning, the tour de force in this delicate operation was to increase the swinging speed of the censer so it's swept along with the quicker and quicker movements you give it so eventually it makes a full circle upside down over the apex, and even then you had to do it discreetly enough, to look natural enough so nobody in the audience notices any mischief and tells the priest about it after the service, and also it was important to take special care not to let the coal fall during the operation, which would have been a highly risky gaffe, when the time came when you'd take the censer in one hand and the incense in the other and go over to the priest, the moment when he'd transform the precious substance into smoke, you had to work things smoothly so he wouldn't be stingy about the amount of incense he dispensed, you had to know how to force his hand, get him to take some more, that's what determined the quantity and thickness of the smoke, and the aroma was sublime, I never wanted it to end, I wished there could be so much that the whole church was plunged in a dense fog, because you see, I've got a weakness for perfume, some women choose their perfumes fantastically well, it's extraordinary when a perfume grips you and you aren't expecting it at all, you come into a room and even before you see the woman sitting there the exquisite odor enfolds you, and also perfume gets rid of bad smells, you know, there're always rotten smells hanging around, gamey, insidious odors, someone needs to air out this old, unhealthy mustiness once and for all, tidy up, draw some demarcation lines, but I'd like to see you try to draw up demarcation lines with all these words bogging your mind down, might as well chase after your shadow in the sun, I can just hear that guy Caracala, life's much simpler than that, he'd say, anyway, look at the real tough guys, they weren't the types to keep re-folding their consciences this way and that, Paris is well worth a mass and my kingdom for a horse, no time for scruples when you're playing quid pro quo, one body give or take isn't the end of the world, you go bury that out in the garden and we can forget about it, Caracala was nuts about crime novels, the part he found thrilling was the mechanism of the story, the thing is, he'd say, the guys who write these are real mathematicians, the whole plot has to be extremely logical, it must be nice to write things like that but I couldn't do it, he added, I've got the imagination but I'm too whimsical, I'd always be wanting to talk about something else, start another story, I'd be more of a wandering artist, and he looked all inspired and dreamy, he swept a lock of hair off his forehead affectedly, yes, I remember that evening well, I can remember the long commentary Cara started to give on the two-bit novels he used to buy at newspaper stands when he went to the city, even today I could clearly describe the café where we were and all the circumstances, because that was the day the evidence suddenly became clear to me with terrible violence, right then it just grabbed me by the throat, of course I'd known for a long time, I'd always known that guy was a sham, but up to that point it hadn't mattered much, it hadn't really affected my friendship with him, then that evening he was talking as usual and the word burst into my head, a sham, buddy, you're nothing but a sham, he didn't have a clue, he was off in the saddle of some story or another, he was probably giving examples of highly-regarded and whimsical crime novels he could have come up with, but for me it was like falling off my horse, you see, I wasn't following him anymore, I no longer wanted to follow him at all, I could see him riding his big words over hill and dale, I wanted to scream stop, stop, that's enough for one day, we can come back to it later, it's time to go home, what a feeling of sadness and deprivation suddenly, but I couldn't have produced a single word, it was stuck inside me, it swept through my whole body and no power in the world could have dragged it out, and right then I stood up, as if a sharp spring had tautened from the soles of my feet to my head, my chair fell over and everyone in the café stopped talking, they turned to see what was happening, and Caracala had to get off his horse, he went silent and looked at me really surprised, it wasas if he'd just woken up with a start, I was standing there, not moving, looking him right in the eyes, and the look we gave each other at that moment must have been the most important look ever in my life, I think we stood there like that for a good minute, and you better believe a minute steeped in that kind of tension feels long, there was a deathly silence and I could see Caracala's eyes start to go misty, I think he got it, I think he could sense the word, that terrible word sham that was dancing through my mind in flaming letters, he could see it in my eyes, still staring at him, then suddenly he had to look away, I left right then, I slammed the door of the café and people must have thought we'd had an argument, and then I walked into the night, straight ahead, and you may not believe it, but I walked like that all night at a terrific speed, without stopping for a second, sometimes I even ran, I wasn't thinking about anything, I needed to feel my muscles working, I needed that feeling of permanent breathlessness, as if walking swept away all the loopy stories Caracala had pulled me into for all those years, as if I had to put all that behind me once and for all, that vast and monstrous swamp of words where I'd been splashing around for so long, that vile yapping he'd kept stuffing into my ears, I had to get away from that for good, and I suddenly thought I'd stick all those words back down his throat one by one, I'd give him a taste of his own medicine, and every step I took was another phrase I flung right in his face, take that, and that and that, and I was walking so relentlessly, and with every step my shoe would hit the ground harder and harder, it was like an entire universe of lies gradually cracking, an enormous weight inside me starting to lift, and that nighttime run was an excellent detox, no more balderdash, never again would I go through life hanging on somebody else's words, then it started raining and I joyfully felt the rain on my burning face, sometime in the small hours that morning I reached the city suburbs, the street where I was walking ran along a park and I went in, in the breaking dawn everything still looked sort of dark green, a little shady, there was a powerful odor of earth and vegetation everywhere, biting, bitter, and irritating, as if the rain falling steadily for the past hour or two had brought up thousands of smells that had been buried in the earth since time immemorial, I pushed my way into a thicket and furiously ripped up the little bushes all around me, some wouldn't come up and I tried with all my strength, I put my whole body into pulling those plants up by the roots, to feel that sudden point when they yield, when they give up all resistance and submit to the grip that kills them, I couldn't stand for a single one to hold out, I had to destroy it all, then I went for a slightly bigger bush than the others, I got totally winded puffing and panting, I was sweating so much it dripped into my eyes so I couldn't see, my whole body was stiff, straining ferociously to uproot that goddamn plant, my whole existence was wrapped up in accomplishing that single task and yet there was no way, the bush held on pitilessly, and through it I saw nature and the entire world taunting me, and then that terrible word came back again only this time it was directed at me, sham, sham, and everything around seemed to echo it, sneering, screaming, and that bush sounded crueler than all the rest, even when I tried one last time with all the strength I had to finally pull it out of the ground, make it obey my law, force it to surrender, there was no way, it was dogged, and stronger than I was, it was jeering at me and I couldn't do anything, and I let go and collapsed on the ground, sobbing, I lay there crying like that for a long time, lying in the mud in the middle of that ravaged thicket, the rage and shame were unbearable, every so often I'd writhe with violent spasms, rolling around on the ground, the whole thing was wretched and ridiculous, and crazy, I'm not sure how long it was before I calmed down and basically passed out, it was the cold that woke me up later, I had to get up, I was staggering, my body and clothes were covered with mud and one of my pants legs was torn from top to bottom, I left the park, people turned to stare as I walked by and I can't even remember how I got home, all I know is it took me several days to talk to anyone, lying in my room most of the time, unable to make sense of my thoughts, to calm down, you know how sometimes it takes a long time to understand how a crisis arose, to grasp the deeper causes and circumstances, there are always a few intangible factors that came up at the last second and played a crucial role, and sometimes it just takes some trifle to set off the disaster, the ground was all ready, but still, without that spark, the fire wouldn't have spread all over the savanna, it's like the fateful straw that breaks the camel's back, or the bow stroke that's slightly too piercing and shatters the crystal glasses, you may notice that in a crisis there's always someone around sniffing for the explosion, who manages to add his two cents' worth, some people love to be the detonators, it's in their blood, they can smell drama simmering from a hundred miles away, so they come running at top speed, they come and ask if they can help out, I don't like those people, they've got a real knack for bringing a problem into full bloom, watering it as needed, bringing the necessary fertilizer, then when it's grown a little, planting it in adequate soil, tying it to a stake, clipping its side branches regularly to keep it growing straight up towards the sky, so it grows into a particularly robust and vigorous problem, and one day it can stand without a stake, you can't control it anymore, it starts mocking you, bending this way and that, making more and more shade, like the tree you plant in front of your window without realizing, and the room gets darker and darker, gloomier and gloomier, dampness creeps in, the wallpaper starts blistering, every day a little more peels off, mold and fungus start growing in all the corners, cracks start spreading across the ceiling, then that gardener with the green thumb for misery sits down and surveys his work with a nasty look, sneering, beware of those people, I was starting to distrust Caracala, too, first of all, as I said, I finally got fed up with all the folderol he'd spout for days and nights on end, and also I got the impression he was probably mixed up in some dirty work, I mean, I don't want to insinuate anything, but just for example, it was weird the way for a few weeks right after Victor was murdered, Cara had so much money, he'd never paid for so many rounds at the bar until then, you kill some Englishman, people asked him, laughing, no, but I inherited some money, he answered with a wink, and then it was a couple more drinks on the left, and a couple more on the right, on and on, and that guy wasn't what you'd call a phony thug, he'd racked up a nice couple of notches on his belt and he had that kind of reputation in the area, when he arrived someplace people got really uneasy, he always carried a knife in his pocket and for no reason at all before you could say boo he had it open in his hand, you didn't want to disrespect him, as he liked to say, I know a few people who paid dearly for it, even at school he was already like a little kingpin, see, I remember he was boss of this group he'd called the Tartars, who were the terror of the schoolyard, always ready to throw a punch, always on the lookout for mischief to perpetrate somewhere in the village, and cunning as Sioux, nobody could ever catch them in the act, I didn't hang around with them, most of the time I stayed at home, I said before I was a loner for a lot of my childhood, I preferred to play by myself or walk through the fields telling myself stories, the one about my real parents, for example, they lived in a big villa with servants, and in this villa they'd set aside two or three gorgeously decorated rooms for me, there was even a canopy bed in the bedroom, in the evening I'd go to bars with my dad, where he'd meet up with friends, in the summer we'd go kangaroo hunting in Australia and they'd let me bring Marie-Ange with us, but it could also turn out that my parents from the city were poor, really poor, and that was the reason they'd placed me with my parents in the village, in that case as soon as they came to get me I brought them good luck, they'd win a fortune or else one night we'd do a fantastic smashandgrab, so in the end it came to the same thing, we had enough to buy a villa and take vacations in Australia, actually the money problem wasn't the most important part of the story, which was the fact that one day I was going to be face-to-face with my truth, all this fog swirling around my life would fade away, my existence would be wonderfully clear, there would be no more lying, one day they'd come with their big black limousine and they might have to kidnap me, I'd be on my way back from school and next to the cemetery the big black limousine would be waiting for me, my parents from the city would be sitting in the back seat and the chauffeur would be standing next to the car, resting his elbow nonchalantly on the hood, when I got close he'd pretend he needed to ask me something, I'd come up without suspecting anything and suddenly he'd stick a chloroform wad under my nose, I'd wake up in my canopy bed, my parents would be at my bedside and they'd explain the whole thing and after a while, you see, I ended up believing so strongly in all these stories that sometimes I seemed to be living two different lives, or else one was reality and the other was fiction, but you'd have to be pretty sharp to say which was which, because when I lived with my parents in town, I didn't believe they were my real parents and I knew I had parents in the village who would come looking for me one day, but still, my heart beat really fast when one day on my way home from school I did actually see a black limousine near the cemetery with the driver waiting by the hood, he was wearing a cap and smoking, and watched idly as I approached, but I knew right away it wasn't the car I'd dreamed about, there were several details that didn't match, a very well-dressed old man came out of the cemetery just as I got to the limousine, the driver very respectfully opened the back door for him and took no notice of me, then he got behind the wheel and the car drove off, I sat down on the grassy bank, I felt all discombobulated, it was as if the whole thing had failed, as if there would never again be a black limousine waiting for me by the cemetery, but at the same time I felt relieved, I can't explain why, but it was like when you've been accused of something and they find out you're innocent, it frees something inside you, a clot that suddenly dissolves, there's nothing more dreadful than a trial, swear to tell the truth, the whole truth, they tell you, ah, it's the boy who cried truth, which is only as good as what you put into it, and yet people always claim they left their nearsightedness in the cloakroom, they never have any doubts, they're sure they saw the defendant prowling around the area a few moments before the murder, but then why are there so many wrongful convictions, why is it they never manage to piece together the whole film of what took place, it's not enough to just trust people, they need to earn it first, although I knew I could trust Marie-Ange, people said some things about her past relationships, but I knew she wasn't the type of girl who'd throw herself at just any guy, and while she may have had a few brief flings before we met, that was no reason to give her the rap, show me one girl who's never had herself a little adventure at some point, but even so, I really didn't appreciate it when Caracala started hovering around her, you know, I could see he'd been trying to bamboozle her with all his fine stories, and also I'd see them together a little too often for my liking, that guy had to get every girl in the bag, of course I knew she didn't listen to his balderdash, it was just that she felt flattered to have that handsome devil Caracala going to such efforts for her benefit, you don't need to be jealous, she'd tell me, Cara's not my type at all, but I noticed he seemed to be avoiding me more and more, when I'd run into him he was always in a hurry, always had someplace he needed to be, we'll meet up next week, he'd say as he hurried by, I've got a juicy job in the works and I don't have a lot of time, anyway the whole thing was pretty shady, it's like one of those stories from the movies where you see the woman stealthily slip a sleeping pill in her husband's cup of tea, and the lover who's come over for dinner gives her a discreet, mischievous wink, the only problem is if you're sitting too close, you might not see the wink because the lover is on the far left side of the screen, so the whole theater bursts out laughing and you're wondering why, you even feel kind of dumb, with my dad it was a sure thing, even if we had good seats, he never got what had happened, he couldn't figure out why people were laughing, basically my dad was always lost at the theater, I think he never really got used to the mobility you get in a film, the almost constantly changing scenery, he'd get confused in the first few minutes, my dad worked hard all week, he fixed fireplaces and heaters, business was good, it was when people started installing central heating everywhere, he'd been in the business for a long time, since he was really young, there was nothing he didn't know about fireplaces and people always called him up when they wanted to build an open hearth, he would have liked me to work with him when I was old enough, we would have done a few years together and then he would have retired and left me the business, but I didn't want to do that, I didn't want anything to do with that job, you've got to think carefully before you choose a profession, I don't know if you pay attention to this type of thing, but every so often there's a story in the newspapers about some fake doctor getting arrested, the guy's been practicing illegally for years, he's got no diploma or maybe he made it himself, and sometimes it's even a surgeon and he's done lots of complicated operations, people said there was nobody else as skilled as he was for peritonitis within a hundred and fifty miles, that all you had to do was look at his hands and you trusted him, and Victor, the guy who lived alone in the fields, his specialty was worms that gnaw at furniture, you know how sometimes you wake up in the night and there's a dull, intermittent little grinding sound, and sometimes it takes weeks to figure out where it's coming from, and then you realize there's a worm crawling around in the oak wardrobe or the walnut laundry cabinet, and I knew people who went half crazy with it, no way they could sleep at night with the worm making so much racket, so they'd get Victor, I think he charged a fair amount but you knew the job would be done right, he'd always find the little beastie in the end, he brought his gear and stayed in the room with the furniture every night, sometimes it took him more than a week to determine the enemy's exact position, you have to realize wood forms a real echo chamber, plus the worm's got its various passageways and it keeps roaming, but Victor had an extraordinary sense for it and when he'd made his calculations, often he only needed to drill one hole to trap the creature and put an end to its voracious and unbearable antics, I've always been fascinated by jobs where there's a secret to discover, a hidden vice to expose, I would have loved to be the detective walking through the garden, for the moment he stays on the main paths, he's still wondering exactly which direction he'll steer his investigations, although with Cara and Marie-Ange it didn't take me long to figure out what was going on, I'd had my suspicions for a while, and I think up to that point I'd been too generous with that guy, because sometimes you end up being swayed by your memory, and memory distorts things, and when you talk about a memory you like to embellish a little, make it sparkle, make it stand out, because basically he said he was my friend but even so he had no problem using the two months when I was in prison to start living with Marie-Ange, no less, that's exactly what happened, the bitch couldn't find anything better to do than move in with him, with all her kit and caboodle, the neighbors werethe ones who told me the truth when I came back, I didn't ask them any

more questions but my blood just boiled and I went over to Caracala's house, you don't take a friend's girl, I said, looking him right in
the eyes, and if you think he looked ashamed, you're right, and I
yelled to Marie-Ange, you've got five minutes to get your things and
come with me, and when we left, I was so furious I grabbed her by the
hair and she had to run along after me like that, half screaming, half
crying, at certain points in your life you can't control yourself, anger
is just boiling through your whole body, it's terrible because you don't
realize what you're doing, you'd kill someone without even realizing
it, my dad was very calm, placid even, sometimes he'd sit in a chair
in front of the house and stay there doing nothing, daydreaming,
everybody needs a little foray into dreamland from time to time,
maybe he was thinking about his fireplaces, too, there's a whole art
to building a chimney that draws perfectly, people in our area said
my dad was kind of a wizard, he knew exactly the right angle to place
the walls, which way the hearth should face relative to the prevailing
winds, there was even a baron who had a chateau in a village nearby
who had my dad restore the big open hearth in his living room, apparently it had been generations since that fire had worked right, you
would have thought there was a curse on the chimney, even if the
wind was favorable and they used really dry wood, it just kept blow-
ing it back and the room got so full of smoke that everyone started
choking and they had to put it out, my dad was working on it for
almost two weeks, on the first day he stood in front of the fireplace
looking at it for several hours, he lit a little fire and tried to figure out
what the problem was, thinking it over with his arms crossed, without moving, I heard that every so often the people in the chateau
came to see what he was up to and they were really struck by how
strange he looked, almost like a seer from what they said, his eyes were
glued to the fire and you would have thought he was dreaming, then
he started measuring and calculating, and he tore out part of the fireplace and rebuilt it, when it was done that was the finest fireplace in
the world, my father had a secret, you see, and people in the business
said he took the secret to his grave, he never wanted to explain to

anybody how he did it, I'm sure he would have told me if I'd agreed to work with him, he often suggested it, he'd say it was a shame to hand such a good business over to some stranger, I would have liked to do it just to please him, but what are you going to do, you can't waste your life just to please your dad, the baron was thrilled with his fully repaired fireplace, years later he would still send us over one or two hares he'd shot when he went hunting, we used to use a skunk to catch rabbits with the farmer next door, first we'd look around to find the warrens and their entrances, then we'd set off with the skunk in a sack, I'd go to one entrance and the farmer would go to another, he'd put the skunk into the warren and the skunk would chase the rabbit out, and all I had to do when it appeared was snatch that future stew and one good blow to the neck, it's not too hard and I can tell you, we filled up the game-bag nicely in an afternoon, I liked that farmer, he knew how to have fun and loved to joke around, but one day a few years later they found him hanging in his attic, a fit of depression most likely, and sometimes you meet people who seem like a barrel of laughs, but when you get to know them you realize deep down they're nursing such a crushing case of neurasthenia it would make the whole world weep, you can't always trust your first impressions, just take Caracala, for example, that guy was always telling stories, with plentiful details, about how he'd been fighting, how he'd beaten so and so up, basically he was always ready with some glib tidbit about brawling, but I'm going to tell you the truth about him, that guy was actually nothing more than a two-bit tin soldier, as far as hanging around alongside the battlefield went, playing at wielding the big guns, strutting on his high horse, sure, that he could do, that's what he was best at, but he wasn't too comfortable actually taking many risks, I know, I told you he'd done one or two crimes, but I suppose I once again got carried away with my story and exaggerated a little, because I'm going to tell you how it really happened that day we tried to steal the old lady's purse, and you can judge for yourself how brave and mighty Caracala was, actually I don't think I told you yet, but we were on a motorcycle that day, our plan was really simple and, in theory, everything should have been easy as pie, Caracala was driving the bike, he was supposed to wait a few yards away with the motor running, I'd snatch the bag really quick and jump on the back, and off we'd go with the loot in hand, the only thing was, and you already heard this, the old lady clung to her purse like the devil to his pitchfork and some passersby came to help, they started hitting me and that's when that bastard Caracala panicked, instead of coming to help me out all he did was ride off at top speed, so obviously I was cooked and you know I got two months for it, don't worry though, the son-of-a-bitch didn't get off scot-free, we met again one day and it was his turn to think about justifying himself, and you better believe he was singing a different tune, old Cara, I couldn't help it, I got scared, he stammered, but there was nothing to explain, you don't clear off when your best friend's in danger, a coward is what he was and I took the opportunity to tell him that, first one to mouth off and first one to turn tail, and since he needed a lesson, I hit him when he wasn't expecting it, right in the stomach and doubled him over, so then I kicked him in the jaw, he fell on the ground half unconscious, I laid into him with a flurry of kicks, it went on and on, that was one hell of a beating, in a few minutes he wasn't moving, there was blood dripping here and there and I felt better, my rage was gone, after all, he'd gotten what he deserved, I always hated cowards, I find cowardice revolting, although I'm very tolerant of other people, I can take most things in my stride, but I can't stand the idea that just because you turn chicken, you'd forget about the most basic expectations of friendship, I was always loyal to people I liked, I always tried to be frank and do what I was supposed to, I'm not saying I never made a mistake, it happens to everyone, but I don't like crafty types who say white and do black, I like people made all in one piece, my mom was like that, in fact, an unbelievably short temper, she'd get angry all the time, but so generous, and it wasn't really her fault she was bad-tempered, she was barely nineteen when I was born, you know, it's hard having children so young, you don't get a chance to enjoy yourself, it's bottles and diapers all day from the beginning so no wonder it's easy to feel bitter, my mom never got to laugh with girls her own age or live carefree, to go for a walk without thinking about a thing, especially since my parents were apparently fairly poor early on, my dad wasn't self-employed yet and my mom had to do housekeeping to make ends meet, they'd known each other forever, they'd almost nursed at the same breast, my dad was an orphan, you see, and my mother's parents took him in, so they were brought up together and got married as soon as they could, I arrived almost right away, my dad loved music and around the time when they got married he was playing the flute in a little orchestra in town, later on he had to stop because he was working too much and they moved to the village, but from time to time he'd take out his flute, he said he'd teach me but I was never very musical, I sing incredibly out of tune for example, people say keep quiet before you make it rain if I get even the slightest inclination to sing a little tune, but I loved singing, it even felt like something I couldn't do without, I knew a bunch of popular songs by heart, I could listen to the radio all evening, I often went out walking by myself in the fields all afternoon, I'd pretend I was a famous singer performing in a recital, and I'd spend the whole walk singing for a crowd of adoring fans, intoxicated with my success, I even went on tour in Australia, it was a smash, I was in all the newspapers, Marie-Ange sent me telegrams every day and we got married when I came back, I'd holler my tunes at the top of my lungs, with all kinds of moves I thought singers probably did on stage, and I remember one time I was so absorbed in my lyrical reverie I didn't realize where I was, only a few steps from the little house where Victor lived, he must have wondered what was happening, who was making so much racket practically right on his doorstep, suddenly I saw him looking at me, where the path turned, I could feel myself going red as a beet and I said hello really awkwardly, trying to act like nothing had happened, he didn't say a word, just touched his index finger to his temple to discreetly indicate what he was thinking, the worst thing in a situation like that is how brutally you fall out of your dream, it was a horrible awakening, the second before, I'd been on stage in Australia, bathed in glory, and then I come to my senses with my croaking voice, acting like a fool unknowingly for one wry spectator, you can understand it was pretty embarrassing, I would have given several years of my life to be able to sing, to be a virtuoso the way I'd planned, I could picture big posters for my recitals, with my name in gigantic letters, then underneath in slightly smaller letters would be that glorious inscription, my magnificent title, that was a profession I could be proud of, virtuoso singer, I held my head high just thinking about it, I could feel myself glowing, to tell you the truth, I've always felt pretty good about myself, it never worried me to think that I was talented and intelligent, and I'd naturally belong to a sort of elite, plus I've never been the shrinking type, when I was after something I can tell you I had no problem going all or nothing to get it, I'm not too fond of shy people, fearful types, in fact here's another example of what Caracala was really like, when we met those sailors in the city, you know the time there was a brawl, that guy Cara was the first one to take cover, you could needle him, even insult him, he'd never rise to the challenge, what happened with the sailors is we were drinking with them at a bar when all of a sudden, I can't remember why, one of them started taunting Cara, and since he was my friend, after all, I couldn't just let it go, I punched the sailor in the face, but don't go thinking Cara helped out in the scuffle, no way, he just stayed in his corner and watched me fighting all three of them, good thing I'm strong as an ox and no way I was going to be frightened of three dudes, even sailors, and then, as I told you, the owner called the police and we cleared out, on the way back Mr. Caracala did look pretty sheepish, I was furious as you can imagine, I didn't say anything for a few minutes and we walked along in silence, I let the mood get a little heavier then I stopped and told Cara to look at me, he looked up anxiously and I socked him one right in the face, there, that'll teach you to be brave, I said, we kept going and he was crying, although to be honest I didn't really blame him, he'd always been like that, when we were kids people in the village made fun of him, they'd say there goes Jean de Nivelle's pooch, he runs away when you call him, when the teacher called on him at school he'd go crimson and start stuttering, it made everybody giggle and the teacher ended up feeling sorry for him and left him alone, he stopped calling on him, I think I told you about this guy named Cram but I don't think I said he was the teacher's son, I can understand it's a fairly ambiguous position to be in, which would have its pluses and minuses, I don't think I would have been exactly thrilled to have my dad as my class teacher, but anyway Cram was my nemesis, so I don't see why I should feel sorry for him, I hated him and he hated me back, so the reason I took Caracala under my wing around that time was he'd become that bastard Cram's whipping-boy, all through recess Cram would terrorize him and it didn't take long before I decided it had to stop, one day Cram was chasing Cara and they passed by me, I put my foot out and sent the pursuer sailing swiftly through the air, and a few seconds later we were rolling around the middle of the play-ground, the whole class was standing around cheering, that little turd had me by the hair and pulled as hard as he could, but I got him in a killer headlock, he started making gagging sounds and stopped pulling so hard, I'd triumphed, except right then I felt someone grab me violently and I got two masterful slaps, it was Daddy to the rescue, if you go after a saint of course God gets annoyed and I paid for it in pages to copy out in detention, I also remember spending the rest of the day kneeling on the platform, and every so often I'd pinch myself to see whether it was by any chance just a dream, and after all that, as you can imagine, Caracala became my faithful friend, in fact we made quite a duo since I was at an age whenI was growing too quickly, I had a crew cut and my big ears stuck out, whereas he was more on the stocky side, and being short-sighted he wore thick glass-es on his round little face, and I haven't told you anything about Marie-Ange for a while, although there's nothing strange about that, after that last story I told you about her things cooled off between us, the thing that bothered me wasn't so much that she'd cheated on me, but that it was with Caracala, I mean really, she could have gone for someone a little better than that, it made her look pretty cheap to have gone and cozied up to that guy, but even so, it was water under the bridge, and in spite of it all, Marie-Ange was still Marie-Ange, end of story, I couldn't do without her, we were riding the same train and couldn't stop midway, in any case that girl did a lot for me, she was the one who taught me to ride a horse, for example, that was her favorite sport, she'd been doing it since she was little and she'd won several prizes in riding competitions, you should have seen her get up to a full gallop in the fields, nobody else could ride a steed through the rough and the smooth like she could, even the most difficult horses did her bidding without any fuss, she had an instinctive harmony with those creatures, a constant shared wavelength, on Sundays she'd take me out on long rides, we'd rent horses from the most established farmer in the village, he had a little business on the side that even attracted customers from the city, my dad's passion was pigeons, there were a couple other people like him in our area, doveys, as people called them, he'd built a big pigeon house in the garden and on Saturday mornings, a courier came to take the birds out for their Sunday race, those charming little creatures had a long way to go, several hundred miles, my dad always had two or three first-class couples, champion birds, on Sunday afternoon he'd wait next to the pigeon house with his whistle, watching the sky, if there was a storm or strong winds sometimes a bird got lost and never came back, on the whole it was pretty unusual, despite the distance a pigeon is always tied to its home, those birds are loyal, I also remember Sunday evenings they used to show films in a bar across from the train station, it lasted only two or three years, but I went there a lot with my parents, there was only one projector and you had to wait while they changed reels, sometimes it took a really long time because the café owner would get irritated, trying to get the projector working, then people used to enjoy getting him worked up on purpose, they'd shout give back our dough, give back our dough, my dad had given me a little theater, you put it together yourself, it was made of cardboard and wood, there were all different kinds of sets and tiny figures for the actors, one day I put on a show for my parents and they couldn't make head or tail of it, my story made no sense and I kept changing sets and characters for no reason, so my dad tried to explain that wasn't how you tell a story but I started crying and wouldn't listen to him, I'm pretty sure I even destroyed my theater after that sad episode, sometimes my dad put me on his lap and told me Bible stories, which were so wonderful I never wanted them to end, my favorite story of all was the flood, I'd always ask for it, I thought Noah was a fantastic character, and the cruise that lasted forty days and forty nights with all the animals on the infinite sea was so perfect that I thought God was an idiot for making the rain stop, one day there was a terrible storm and a horse was struck by lightning in a meadow about a hundred yards from our house, as soon as I heard I ran over to the horse, he had a wide burn all the way down his back, the farmer had gone into town that day, nobody'd thought to put him in the stable and when the storm started we heard him whinny but it was too late, he was dead within seconds, I'll tell you, I've never seen a sadder sight than a dead horse, and this one was a noble, magnificent creature, like the ones that sometimes went trotting through my dreams, my happy dreams, that is, because the others were inhabited by less pleasant animals and jaunts, for example, did you ever dream a crocodile's chasing you, because despite its looks a crocodile can run really fast, it's more fleet-footed than you'd expect at first glance and I'd just like to see you with a crocodile ready to chomp down on your hindquarters if you don't pick up the pace, as it happens I also used to dream about a short, skinny man who walked around with a crocodile-skin briefcase, he was bald with a fine white beard, he was waiting for me at every turn demanding that I hand over some papers I didn't actually have, you'll never get away with this, he'd bellow, stop telling tales and give me the papers, I know what you wrote, I've got evidence, do you hear me, and he'd nervously light a cigarette, they should make films of people's dreams, light, vaporous stories, nightmares where a heap of papers keeps growing and growing as a little man counts them feverishly, I also really like films that suddenly show a character's dream, the image goes fuzzy or there's a sort of halo of smoke around the actors, for me dreams are like the sirens' song or the deep, mesmerizing voice of Fate, yes, it's a voice from another world, although when I was living with my town parents, I dreamed a lot less, maybe because of the atmosphere there, my town parents were very serious, my dad had a big office with lots of books lining the walls, that was where he'd meet important people who came to the house in limousines nearly as big as his, from time to time he summoned me to his office to talk about my future, as for my mom I didn't see her much, she travelled a lot and went to visit friends, so sometimes I'd get bored and decide to go spend some time in the country, especially since I knew more people in the village than in the city, but there were some people I didn't trust, and I think probably with good reason, take Caracala, I'm sure that guy never really had a clean conscience, the look on his face wasn't honest, and if you looked right at him he'd start blushing right away, one time he started telling me a weird story, something about a stolen flute, but he alluded to it only through veiled hints, I knew not to rush him, or ask overly direct questions, so I tried to discreetly and skillfully work the details out of him, just little by little, taking care not to spook him, but his answers were full of contradictions, the more he explained, the more muddled and upset he got, and in the end he wouldn't say another word, well from then on I lost whatever trust I still had in him, I knew I had good reason to avoid hanging around with him, that guy had to be a pervert, he wasn't very popular with the ladies so he'd manage with the waitresses at the Tabarin, that was his constant haunt, who knows where he got the money for it, hanky-panky at the Tabarin didn't come cheap, I can tell you, though everyone's got something a little dubious up their sleeves, why don't you spend an hour or two scouring your conscience and see what kind of gems emerge, I'd love to hear the results of your little introspective reverie, I'm not sure you'd keep looking at me so sincerely and candidly, I should let you know nobody's better than I am at getting to the core of the problem, opening up the cut that won't heal properly, I knew what was what right away when Marie-Ange told me she'd miscarried, I knew she was lying and why she'd disappeared for several days, I just didn't push the issue, I knew it would just lead to another massive fight and in any case you might say I wasn't too directly involved in the situation, I never wanted to bring it up again after that, but that's also because I don't like drama, I hate what they refer to as psychological conflicts or any other nonsense like that, you only get one life and you have to make the most of it, my dad knew that, he did what he pleased and was happy like that, forget about tormenting his mind with all kinds of problems, he had his fireplaces and chimneys during the week and his pigeons when he came home, he didn't ask for anything from life, that was enough, that guy Caracala came over one day and asked shyly whether my dad could teach him about keeping pigeons, he wanted to build a pigeon house at his place and buy one or two couples when he saved up some pocket money, my old man was really pleased as you can imagine, especially since I could never stand those creatures and he couldn't talk to me about them, they're always cooing and cuddling, all I wanted to do was wring their necks, and you should have seen those two idiots with their pigeons all day long Saturday and Sunday, after a month or two my dad gave a couple to Caracala and he won the first race he entered his pigeon in, it arrived half an hour before the others, Cara was as proud as Artaban, at the same time it was pretty handy for my dad to have a pupil, Cara could deal with all the dirty work, he'd clean the muck out of the pigeon house for example, me, I'd done that once just to be nice to my dad and I swore never again, I'd figured it out, but you shouldn't think I have an aversion to physical tasks, it's just that even back then I was attracted to loftier activities, I liked our neighbor, the farmer, the widow of the guy who ended up hanging himself, she played piano, she came from a bourgeois family in the city and brought her instrument with her when she got married, I don't think her family was thrilled with her choice, either, marrying a farmer is a step down, but I think that was during the war, so it was really useful for provisions, also with the farm work she ruined her hands and couldn't play as well as before she got married, she didn't have much time either, but

I still loved going and listening to her, as soon as she sat down at the piano her sense of grandeur came back and I would always ask her to play A Maiden's Prayer, I was fascinated with that piece because to play it requires crossing your hands on the keyboard several times, if I remember correctly, it's the right hand that has to go searching for several notes way down in the bass notes, at the time that gesture seemed to me like the height of virtuosity, the music flowed like a river, it slipped and slipped, and kept slipping and I let myself slip into the infinite with it, the thing I can't stand is when I'm listening to music I love and suddenly realize it's coming to the end, the piece is nearly over, it's stupid how there's always an ending, you know, I hate endings, I can't stand them, they make my skin crawl, it's the same thing with films, by the way, you should be able to watch films that are a year long, for example, someone could come feed you regularly, with a break from time to time to sleep, can you imagine, going to buy your ticket for a whole year of dreaming, with that you could stuff your dome nicely for sure, but there's never time to get your fill, one time I saw a mare in a field, young and twitchy, and beautiful as well, she was standing near the fence bordering the next field, without moving, looking rather innocent, as if you shouldn't get too close to her, and in the next field was a stallion about to lose his marbles, the poor beast, his piece kept getting longer and longer underneath him, he'd back up and gallop towards the fence but it was too high and he had to stop every time, he'd wait a little while, dejectedly, then start all over again, but the most fascinating thing was how still the mare was, she didn't move a hoof, I stood there watching for more than an hour and she never made a peep, and on the other side of the fence the stallion was wearing himself out running towards the fence, he became more and more frenzied, life is full of frustrations like that and people enjoy adding more of them, they put fences up everywhere, put photos in frames, put their lives in order, you know how obsessive types live their lives, there was a guy in the village like that, he had seven pipes and every day of the week he smoked a different one, when you'd run into him all you had to do was look at which pipe he had in his mouth to tell which day it was, I can hear you objecting though, saying people wouldn't necessarily have known which pipe corresponded to which day, and I'll have you know I've never been able to stand hair-splitters, and so I've decided from now on I'll tell whatever stories I feel like telling, and I'm not deaf either, I know my own talent as a storyteller, I never needed to walk around with pebbles in my mouth to learn how to talk, I know when I start speaking people aren't averse to coming and listening, and the truth is I've always enjoyed being the center of attention when I'm someplace, I feel flattered by the role, that's why I really liked walking with crutches, you remember the story of the beet, when that German shepherd had bitten me neatly in the leg, well for several weeks afterwards I was walking with crutches, I can tell you using those things is better than wearing a crown, everyone let me go first, they'd rush over to help me, at school someone would always go hang my crutches up on the coat rail and get them for me when class finished, even the teacher looked at me with respect and Cram was dying of jealousy, plus those crutches were my bodyguards, I felt all powerful between them, I could defend myself, you wouldn't dare disrespect me despite my injury, and when the injury healed all too quickly, I kept walking with crutches for quite a while, and it was a dark day when I had to stow them away in a wardrobe, I always liked to have a sense of support, Caracala was kind of like my servant, I'd send him here and there, he did everything he could to please me, he was a bit of a halfwit, too, I'd read a particularly suggestive description of a great king's court and it gave me the idea to make Cara into my jester, the role suited him to a T and he accepted it gratefully, every so often I'd sit down and say in a noble voice, now amuse me, then he'd start clowning around, he pulled unbelievable faces and even got down on all fours and barked like a little pooch, then I called him and gave him a sugar cube, there was only one thing he was incapable of in his role as jester and that was keeping me amused by telling a story, he'd tried several times but the poor guy, see, he had absolutely no imagination and his stories were totally boring, I might note in passing that I was far more talented than he was in this area, in any case after a couple of minutes I was bored stiff, so I ordered him to go back to his dog position, I would have liked to get a dog but my dad was against it, he said it would eat up all his pigeons, it was an old bone of contention between him and my mom, when she was younger she'd had a poodle and she wanted to get another one, I told you before, my parents got married very young, yes, of course I know the stories people told but I'm absolutely certain they weren't true, they said my mother knew she was pregnant when she met my dad and pulled the wool over his eyes so I could have a father, people even said I looked a little too much like old Victor but people talk all kinds of nonsense, they just talk for the sake of talking and bad mouthing other people behind their backs, because every family has some redheads, and just because Victor was a bit redheaded doesn't prove anything, I don't like the way I look, they called me carrot at school, and the color makes you stand out immediately, it's impossible to be anonymous, when we attacked the old lady and took her purse we ran like jackrabbits and it was a done deal, only she told the police that one of the attackers had red hair and the next day those goddamn coppers came looking for me at home, my mom was really great, when the police rang the bell she knew I was in for some trouble, so she told them I wasn't there and said it loud enough so I could hear, I was in the kitchen and tried to slip out through the garden, but there were two policemen hiding behind the cemetery wall and I got caught, my mom had always known I didn't want to take the same path as everybody else, she'd tell me, son, enjoy yourself while you're young, she even took my side against my dad when he criticized me for one escapade or another, after my two months in prison Marie-Ange told me she was pregnant, it struck me as really strange because I realized right away she was fudging the dates a bit, we had a serious argument, I got angrier and angrier, I couldn't stand the idea that she'd lie like that but it wasn't true what people said, I didn't hit her that night, and in any case she'd decided not to keep the baby, that was when she got a job in the city, we didn't see each other much because she'd rented a room there and only came back to the village every so often, it was too tiring to go back and forth in the train every day, especially since Marie-Ange had never been very strong physically, and maybe I was never really that fond of her, you know how falling in love gets your imagination all worked up, just because she flashes you a smile you immediately start convincing yourself you've found the rare pearl, sometimes I even thought Marie-Ange was the one, but I don't think we would ever have managed to be happy together, to build something that would last, basically the relationship flattered me because she was the prettiest girl in the village, yes, when I think about it, it was a kind of pride I felt rather than true love, maybe true love is something that only happens in the movies, it's a dream, it makes plenty of smoke but smoke fades quickly, it's true people are frightened of reality and they're ready to swallow anything as long as it helps them forget, a fairytale, a morsel of dream, anything goes as long as it's something other than what they're going through at the moment, well I, in any case, have no hesitation saying these practices are dangerous, we think all those stories we make up are innocuous but my own experience demonstrates how untrue that is, sometimes fiction overflows into reality and it's a disaster, if you need an example here's a good one, you remember my little games with Caracala, he was my jester and did whatever I told him to, one day I told him, same as usual, I want to hear a story, the king wants a story from his joker's lips, so he sat down at my feet and started trying to come up with a story, and since he wasn't too clever, the more it went on the more bogged down he was, I made fun of him and insulted him, kings always do that with their jester, and he took my teasing and insults with his head down, now you can go on, I said, he started back on his story but I stopped him right away to point out how stupid and senseless it was, he did his best to carry on and I was sniggering the whole time, joker, your story's the pits, it's not worth a red cent, it's not worth wearing out my eardrums listening to it, come on now, show me you can do better than that, his voice kept trailing off more and more, he was making a huge effort to continue but eventually the sobs drowned out his words, I got up and gave him a kick, come on, jester, tell it, tell it, finally he got up too and left without looking back, he was crying hot tears, the innocent game had crossed a line somewhere, I didn't see Caracala until I got to school the next day and he avoided me for several days, afterwards we never talked about what happened and we never played king and jester again, but from then on he started stammering more and more, he even got quite a reputation in the area, people would laugh and imitate the way he talked and if they didn't understand what someone was talking about because it was muddled, because it ended with a tangle of explanations, they'd say enough Caracala tales, I know vultures always circle the fallen, but his reputation just got worse and worse, in the end whenever people talked about Cara he was practically like the village idiot, he should have tried his luck somewhere with friendlier skies, one word I always really liked was loot, it makes you think of a party, of something magical, bring the loot, pass the loot, there's the loot, it makes you picture a big sack full of gold pieces, a nice round sack, that word's stuffed with poise and good cheer, I like to use words like that when I talk, put them on a throne in the middle of my speech, it's like scribble or babble, they're juicy words, they make your mouth water when you pronounce them, it makes me smile to think about how Caracala babbled or how badly Cram fumbled at fishing, because I can tell you, that idiot Cram spent entire days fishing and almost never caught anything, once I read in the newspaper that they'd arrested a guy who was selling blotting paper that erased spelling mistakes, he was selling his merchandise door-to-door and it was a good little business, people need someone to make them believe things like that exist and I'm sure the guy cheered everyone up in their cottages, so many people live in terror of writing to their superiors because of spelling issues, but in the end some grouch complained, he must have realized those blotting papers didn't work all that well, you may have noticed that's how it always ends up when you bluff your audience, it starts with the prophet's flute and ends with the hangman's drum, one time I was sick for

several weeks and I couldn't go to school, I lost weight, I had a constant fever, my parents called the doctor several times but he couldn't
see what was wrong, since I still had a good appetite and kept losing
weight, they finally realized I had a tapeworm, the awful thing was
when my mom tried to catch it, they didn't give me any food all day
to do it, I had to hold my mouth open over a bowl of warm milk and
my mother was there ready to grab the worm, but the enemy could
sense danger and refused to take the bait, it made me retch horribly,
it's terrifying to spend all day with a bug inside you, once I knew it
was there I could feel it wriggling all the time, whatever I ate just went
to feed it and it drained all my energy, and as time went by it grew and
grew, and sometimes it felt as if that monster was invading my whole
form, my body no longer belonged to me, I was harboring an enemy
who fed on my blood, my life was only a vehicle for the parasite, my
existence just helped it grow and become even more enormous and
demanding, the day would come when it would be so gigantic that
I'd choke to death, but it would keep feeding on me until my death
rattle and the only consolation was that my death would kill it as
well, but even that wasn't completely certain because I imagined it
might be able to slip out, I pictured my body lying on the ground
and from my half-open mouth a fat white worm, sticky and fantastically long would slide out of me and glide coolly away, as the end
appeared on the screen and the lights coming back on in the theater
would show the nauseated faces of the few viewers who'd had the
guts to stay till the end, Caracala couldn't stand the sight of blood, it
made him faint, he couldn't help it, just one drop and he was out of
commission, you wouldn't have wanted to ask him to go help someone wounded in the road, so you can understand when the police
came looking for him because two young thugs had killed an old
lady, it was clear from the start we were dealing with a miscarriage of
justice, that guy wouldn't have hurt a fly, I remember they put him
in handcuffs and he refused to go along, he was protesting his inno-
cence, I didn't do anything, I didn't do anything, let me go, he was
shouting, nobody dared to intervene because you know how people

don't like to get involved in situations like that, it can blow up in your face, me, I've always kept in the habit of minding my own business, that's always suited me up to now and I can tell you I have no intention of changing policy anytime soon, it's also true that I won't have people coming and nosing around in my things or telling me to justify myself, that's why I found it hard to live in the village, people are always busy checking out their neighbor's pile of straw, and if you could have seen the chair attendant ladies gossiping on the corner in the summer, one time it got on my nerves so badly that when I saw a big group of them all together I ran towards them screaming at the top of my lungs and they scattered, away went those dirty things in their black robes, though they were back five minutes later flapping their chins, almost the same thing happened another day, I got in a rage, I was yelling all through the house and my mom was overwhelmed, I was grabbing anything I could see, vases, plates, I was wreaking havoc, then I took my dad's gun down from where it was hanging on the wall, my mom covered her face with her hands, she thought I was going to kill her, but I went out and when I saw the flock of geese at the farm next door I fired, I shot three of them, I couldn't help it, I just couldn't stand those creatures, afterwards when I'd calmed down I went and apologized, I even paid them for the dead geese, the farmer wanted to call the police but his wife talked him out of it, she liked me a lot, occasionally when she had time we'd go and do charcoal sketches in the fields, in fact she's the one who first introduced me to hanky-panky, she was really beautiful and one day when we were sketching a landscape I felt her hand stroking my neck, a second later we were lying in a thicket, although for hanky-panky no girl could top Marie-Ange, nobody held a candle to her, she'd go more and more, and our rides went on and on, one time, we'd been in the saddle like that for quite a while, we'd taken refuge in a cluster of trees that belonged to the baron, the one with the open fire, suddenly we heard a voice behind us and knew it was time to clear out, it was the baron's gamekeeper, aren't you ashamed of behaving yourselves that way in the baron's woods, he says to us, you little perverts are going to frighten off all the game, I really think that man was half nuts, he was angry as a hornet, he was pointing his gun at us and he even started kicking us, I got a kick in the ribs and since I was completely naked I didn't take too kindly to it, so I leaped up, grabbed the gun by the barrel and tore it from his hands, then I hit him sharply on the head with the butt and down he went, a voice in the shadows jeers, I hear it cruelly murmuring, you dumb jerk, now you've got another body on your hands, well let me tell you I take full responsibility for that body, after all I was acting in self-defense, that nutcase could have killed Marie-Ange and me, and when the police came to get me the next day I went with my head held high, I wasn't scared of the trial or the judges, I'd be able to explain how insane that man was, you should have seen all the witnesses they brought out, Marie-Ange, my parents, Caracala, Victor, the farmer and his wife, my aunt, the baron and even Cram, who the prosecution had called in, as I'd predicted I was acquitted, no, that body wasn't enough to put me away, the unexpected arrival of the gamekeeper was just an episode that ended badly, nothing more, all that remains is to kick away the ladder, look around somewhere else after that accident, because life is full of accidents, we never know what tomorrow will bring and age breaks even the strong man, as they say, the trick is always to start off again, to get your horse back on the road, off we go, off we go, I've often dreamed of those grand, bright mornings when you see the voyager stroke his horse's neck as he watches the horizon, onwards, ever onwards, don't try to grasp why he neither rests nor pauses, why he's always on the road, he probably couldn't tell you himself, he has perpetual motion somewhere in his belly, it's like Don Juans, another woman, and one more, and each new woman is as important as the last, and every time they'd risk their lives for it, look at the wandering Jew, the ghost ship, they're the same kind of story, there's always something beckoning you elsewhere, creepy-crawling on you, I like unsettled people, who don't know where they're from and don't know where they're going, at the same time I don't like people who know too much, detectives, always walking around with a magnifying glass on well-maintained garden paths, like my town parents' garden, you should have seen the groves, the flowerbeds, the statues, I remember being dressed in a sailor suit and playing with a little girl named Marie-Ange, she had blond braids and big green eyes that took up most of her face, and when I think about that garden it makes me uneasy, all my childhood anxieties rise to the surface, over by the back wall was a place I wouldn't have gone near for anything in the world, it was a little shed where the gardener stored his tools and next to it was a pile of dead leaves he was turning into compost, I used to terrorize Marie-Ange by telling her there was a body buried there, this Marie-Ange from the village, her dad was the stationmaster, I realize it's a respectable profession but that was still no reason to think she was born from Jupiter's thigh, always giving me a hard time by claiming I was poorly dressed, that I had no upbringing, that I didn't know how to behave in polite company, finally I said to her that's enough, your ladyship, don't think I'm going to worry about your moods, if I'm not your type you can just find someone else, my parents raised me quite freely and they weren't too concerned about etiquette, meals were pretty no-fuss at our house, when there were no clean dishes left we'd wash a couple and that was fine, in the village people thought we were weirdos, they called us the cranks next to the cemetery, when I was old enough my dad showed me how to set snares in the woods, because as it happened, poaching was his passion, as much as the baron's gamekeeper tried to keep watch he never managed to collar him, ah, you should have smelled the aroma in the kitchen on certain days, we had some fine stews at the baron's expense, my mom may not have been too tidy but you would have had to run a long way to find a cook in her league, one day the police came looking for my dad, the day before he'd come home with a dirty face as if he'd been fighting and I'd been sent to bed really early that night, my dad went to prison, my mom cried a lot but he wasn't gone for long, he kissed both of us and looked at us victoriously, it doesn't matter, he said, they didn't find the loot, a few days later some people from town came to see my parents, a really

PAUL EMOND

elegant couple, the man was wearing a brandspanking new suit and
extremely high-fashion Italian shoes, the woman was radiating some
heady perfume, they got out of a big black limousine and the driver
stayed outside waiting for them, he was pacing along the cemetery
wall smoking a cigarette, they told me to go play somewhere else, and
I was fascinated with rich people, my parents didn't normally hang
around with people like that, they stayed at least a good two hours
and the driver got more and more impatient, I never found out what
that conversation was about, no one would tell me, but for a little
more than a month my dad's face seemed worried, he was very affec-
tionate with me, he cuddled me, it seemed like he was afraid of losing
me, then one day he came home extraordinarily excited, he said a
waitress at the Tabarin had been killed the night before, half the
building had burned down and in a bedroom they'd found the rich
visitor with the big limousine that had fascinated me so much a few
weeks before, my dad burst out laughing and talked on and on, even
though he was normally the silent type, my dad, and a bit of a philosopher, too, he'd often go out walking alone in the fields and that
must have been his time to refine his idea of the world, to think about
the meaning of life, people for miles around considered him wise and
when anyone in the village had some moral dilemma they'd often
come to him for help, the priest hated him because he thought he
was stealing his customers, my dad had the physique of an ascetic, a
thin, craggy face with machete-cut features and a fine grey beard that
he always stroked when he was thinking, he was a confirmed atheist,
he even liked to go to the village butcher's on Good Friday to buy
some chops and specifically say they were for our dinner, that might
seem banal nowadays but I can tell you at the time it caused a serious
uproar, people predicted that God would take his revenge and my
dad would die a violent death, because back then people fasted all
through Lent and the priest had the congregation at his beck and
call, although I never really believed in that man's holiness, Marie-
Ange had been his servant and told me he had roving hands, men are
men, after all and the poison's in the prick, as they say, therefore I

don't see why certain people should be denied their hanky-panky, I've always found those particular human categories surprising, people who aren't like everyone else, priests, hermits, or crazy people, maybe deep down all those people aren't as bizarre as they seem at first sight, just take Caracala for example, between you and me I'm not sure that guy was as crazy as people claimed, I mean, I know he was a bit simple, but you also have to recognize he obeyed his own logic, in a way, he lived in his own universe, which had a certain coherence, I even think in his own way Cara was happy, you'd see him strolling through the village streets with his dog who followed him everywhere, he was always walking around with several days' worth of stubble and his clothes were so filthy it looked as if he'd rolled around in the dirt, everyone felt sorry for him, we'd give him a little change sometimes and when he passed in front of our house, my mom would bring him a bowl of soup on the doorstep, one winter evening I met him in front of the cemetery, he was laughing softly with his odd laugh, there was a little saliva around the corners of his mouth, I could tell he'd just seen the will-o'-the-wisps and was thrilled about it, he even clapped his hands together and mumbled some incomprehensible words, I think I told you that Marie-Ange had worked in town for quite a while, if I remember right she got the job a few weeks after refusing to work anymore for the priest, she claimed that one evening he hadn't stopped at a few stealthy gropes but had tried to force her door and get into bed with her, after that incident the priest was transferred somewhere else by the diocese and another one assigned in his place, the problem, you see, is I'm not sure how far we can trust Marie-Ange's statements, that girl was really nice but she was still a bit of a compulsive liar, as for the story I told you, I'll admit I never found out exactly what happened but let's just say it wasn't the first time she'd said things that were questionable at best, for example, one time she claimed someone had attacked her when she was walking by the cemetery and that she'd nearly been raped, and the fact is they never found the slightest sign of an attacker, in any case, as I was saying, she got a job in town, she left early in the morning and came back late in the evening and we didn't see each other much, but when she had time on Sundays, she'd come over to sew with my mother, Marie-Ange loved to be in on secrets and I enjoyed telling them, there are stories I've never told anyone else, she's the only person who knows me through and through, it was a pleasure to watch Marie-Ange and my mother working together under the lamp, it gave the room a feeling of peace and tranquility, my dad was sitting in his armchair, smoking a huge cigar and every so often casually knocking the ash off, I was reading a crime novel, that was my favorite thing, you know those two-bit novels you buy in train stations and newsstands, often I hadn't even come to the middle of the book before I figured out the key to the mystery, although most of the time it wasn't all that clever, first the detective has to find the body, once he finds it he'll automatically deduce who the killer is, that isn't always the exact story but nine times out of ten it's pretty close, it doesn't take a genius to put together a crime mystery, you come up with a story set in a garden, set it up so the detective's investigations progress logically towards the back wall, put in a bit of mischief in the shrubbery with a definite whiff of hanky-panky, and there you go, sometimes I got tired of reading and went out for a walk even if it was raining, because I don't know if I told you but I love the rain, especially a heavy rain with big raindrops that whip down onto your face, that was one of my greatest pleasures, taking off like that on a rainy afternoon and just wandering around, without a destination, I could feel the dampness gradually soaking through my clothes and it gave me a boost, sometimes I'd go find Caracala and we'd walk together, he was simple-minded, sort of a village idiot, but he was gentle and calm and deep down I liked him, plus since he was deaf and dumb he didn't get on your nerves, I think he really enjoyed those long walks, we'd go through the fields side by side, sometimes he'd gesture to show me something, a rabbit scampering off or horseback riders in the distance, or sometimes a carrier pigeon high in the sky, I really enjoyed helping my dad look after his pigeons, I think they're incredible little creatures, when my dad and I lost one in a race it was as if someone had taken one of our family, we were overwhelmed with sadness, my dad was a big softy and he'd get teary-eyed at the drop of a hat, at funerals in the village people always thought it must be a close relative of his, he looked so stricken, so you can imagine when I did my two months in prison because of the old lady's bag, he was beside himself with sorrow, he was wringing his hands, when I came back he asked why would you do something like that, son, why'd you do it, but I promised I'd never do it again and he forgave me right away, I was always a well-behaved child, I was the best pupil in my school, the other kids called me Cram, who knows why, at home I was normally the one who looked after the garden, next to the cemetery wall I'd built a little shed to store my tools, at my town parents' house, though, I was unruly and I had my reasons to be, if you'd met my town dad you would have realized it couldn't be any other way, that man never made a move he didn't need to, he never spoke an unnecessary word, he spoke curtly to the servants, he called my mom my dear one or else my dear, his life was as precise as a fine watch and he expected everyone else in the house to live the same way, so I was always looking to cause him some trouble, I'd go into his office when he wasn't around and take some random papers out of the files on the table, tear them up, and bury them out in the garden, I'm sure it must have set him back at work because sometimes he looked even more surly than usual, or even kind of worried, or he'd interrogate the servants, but those good people had no reason to steal papers like that, my mom tried to keep to the rhythm, sometimes she'd feel weak, then she'd stop walking back and forth through the house and scolding the servants, she'd lie down on a couch and stay there without moving for hours, you could see the tears in her eyes, she was a lot younger than my dad and sometimes it was hard to for her to accept such a serious life, I actually think she would have preferred to live with me in the village, but it was impossible, you see, it would have been too complicated, complete bedlam night and day, one day I was at the movies and they were showing a detective film, it was a really exciting one, the detective was looking for some lost papers, he was short and bald and was after the hero who walked around everywhere with the papers hidden in a crocodile-skin briefcase, everyone was glued to the screen, wondering how it was going to end, when all of a sudden we found ourselves in a Western, the second before we had been watching the detective spying on the hero in the pathways of big garden and the next second the screen was filled with riders galloping through the dust, there was a general shudder of disgust in the audience, people started screaming and they stopped the film, the lights came on and after that the theater manager came in very embarrassed, he explained there'd been a mistake, a Western reel had somehow slipped in instead of the last reel of the detective film, of course they'd refund our ticket prices, he apologized to the viewers and appreciated their kind understanding, but the audience didn't take it kindly at all, there were boos, jibes, and generally people getting completely furious, you've got no right to do something like this, they yelled, it's immoral, some people were asking the manager how the film ended, but he had to admit he had no idea because it was the first time he'd seen the film, too, they're trying to make fools of us here, screamed an old lady, but believe me when I say the angriest one there was yours truly, I could have strangled that theater manager, I remember going straight up to him, looking him right in the eye, and telling him, with all the scorn I felt for him, you sir are an irresponsible person, then I left because I didn't want to do something I'd regret, I calmed down a little by walking through the streets, but you can bet I won't forget that story anytime soon, the manager could have at least taken the trouble to check the reels before the film started, when people come to see a show they're looking for pleasure and they pay for it, so for me it's criminal to cut you off at the best part, it would be like the waiter suddenly coming and taking your plate just before you bit into the best part that you'd saved for the end, or if a waitress at the Tabarin jumped off the couch before the romp was over, I used to go there a lot, especially when Marie-Ange was working, it made my mother cry because she said it was a den of iniquity, but even the little red lights in the windows behind the curtain got me excited, and Marie-Ange liked me, I was even her favorite client and when I arrived there she always welcomed me with a big smile, she smoked Egyptian cigarettes and I'd follow her into the little lounge, there was a really comfortable sofa and rugs covering the floor, at my town parents' house there were also lots of rugs, my dad collected paintings and art objects, in the middle of the living room there was a big painting of a woman in a long dress sitting at the piano, she was looking at herself in a mirror positioned in the background of the painting and you could see her face only in the mirror, it looked detached from her body, I would have liked it if the woman came to life, and you suddenly saw her smile as she started playing A Maiden's Prayer, in the corner of the room there was also a sort of statue, it was a woman's body without a head, a slightly obese and mutilated trunk, strangely white with an open stomach giving birth to a disjointed keyboard that somehow seemed to invite you, and then further on, on a console table, was a big jade crocodile that one of my dad's clients, a rich publisher, had given him when he came back from a trip to Oceania, it was a marvelous beast, the scales shone like gold and its tail quivered in the light, I loved that crocodile, it was my idol, my secret god, and at night I'd come silently down to the living room to entreat it, it had strange eyes that you could hardly see but always seemed to be laughing, one day a servant dropped it while she was dusting and the crocodile ended up in the trash, the following Sunday my parents and I went for a ride in the big black limousine, I'm not sure what happened but the driver got distracted and we drove into a plane tree, I was the only survivor, I was in the hospital for two months and I still had to walk on crutches for a long time afterwards, one day I went to the village, I went limping into a bar, sat down, and leaned my crutches next to me, it seems like just yesterday, there were two customers there, one was sitting at the table across from mine and by coincidence, he had his leg in a cast and also crutches sitting next to him, he gave me a weird look, smiling and grimacing at the same time, he had several days of stubble and filthy clothes, he made a little gesture that I didn't understand

and just as I was going to speak to him the other customer, who was sitting at the counter chatting with the lady who owned the place, turned to me, he said don't bother talking to Caracala, he's a deaf-mute and, you know, a bit simple, anyway he wouldn't understand what you're saying, but don't worry, he's not dangerous, and with that the customer got off his stool and came over to sit down at my table, he explained that this poor guy Caracala had been bitten really badly, right to the bone by a German shepherd that belonged to one of the farmers in the village, and what was strange was the farmer had been found hanged in his attic a few days later, he was pretty nice, this guy telling me all these stories, he said his name was Victor, I don't come to the village too often, he added, I live out in the fields and that suits me, since it was only early afternoon I stayed in the bar for quite a while, I drank a lot with Victor, then we went on to some more places, with the result that by the middle of the night I was completely drunk and fell asleep in a ditch, in the morning, unfortunately, the police were passing right by there and found me and brought me home, my mother was screaming, haven't you brought enough shame on us already, haven't you, my mother yelled a lot, but the fact is, she needed to, once she got started it was better not to try to interrupt, better to let her go through her whole litany, afterwards she seemed relieved, she'd calm down, although one day she got terribly angry and in contrast to what usually happened this was a concealed, silent anger, which made a much bigger impression, it was a real change from her usual yelling, my dad had gotten drunk with some other guys from the village and then they'd gone to the Tabarin, then the neighbors went and told my mom, her blood started to boil, she got her coat and umbrella, and went to find my progenitor, they came back half an hour later, my dad was staggering but hanging his head and my mom didn't say anything, her lips were pursed and she didn't open her mouth for a week, let me tell you, my old man was sure nice that week, it was a real change from his usual tyrannical attitude to the household, when he came home from work it was bring me my slippers and the paper, if there wasn't any beer I could run and buy him some, my mother submitted to him about everything, she was a real slave, poor woman, she had to yield to every little whim of her master and lord, one fine day she had enough, she packed her suitcase, and we never saw her again, I was really sad and it caused a huge scandal in the village, but I completely understand, I'd even say she should have done it a lot sooner, I was fourteen at the time and my dad and I lived together, just the two of us, after that, it wasn't much fun because my dad got really depressed about what happened, fortunately I fell in love with Marie-Ange not long afterwards, that girl kept my spirits up when I was young, always in a good mood, always a smile on her face, and no prude, either, she was an outspoken type and you could forget about putting her in her place unless you were pretty sharp, I liked it when she told me about her dreams, they were always full of fantastic palaces and extraordinary adventures, but I think they probably weren't her real dreams that she told me, she must have invented a lot of it, you see Marie-Ange loved telling stories, she sort of lived in another world, me, I've always been partial to realism, for me dreams are just old wives' tales that will never get you anywhere, just a waste of energy, a muzak ditty, which is why in the end I had enough of Marie-Ange, and also I was always restless when it came to hanky-panky, back then I was cock of the walk, I had to get all the girls, one after the other, I was insatiable, and I don't mean to brag, but I have to say I did pretty well, I was unstoppable at the Saturday night dance, the other thing was I had a way with words, I always had a few good lines up my sleeve to bring down the walls of Jericho, and apparently there was nobody else as handsome as I was within fifteen miles, I loved dancing, I was a born dancer, and I'm sure I could have become famous at ballet, whenever I heard any music I couldn't help it, my legs started itching and I had to dance, I made up the boldest and wildest steps, I whirled across the floor like a frenzied weathervane, my partner had to hang on properly, nothing else could get her dizzied up like our rhythmic little jaunt, I won the contest for best dancer at every dance, the girls would argue over who would get to dance with me, I enjoyed having everyone stop to watch me as I performed with my partner, I had the whole floor to myself, it was intoxicating, but I was modest despite my glory, I was always a modest type, I never liked to put myself in the spotlight too much, I think it's unhealthy and that you shouldn't draw attention to yourself, I've never shouted look at me, look at me, I can't stand show-offs, the little guys with brand new suits, always ready to exaggerate, puff their necks out, ham it up, it's all just smoke and nothing else, blow on it and there's nothing left, it's like those people who have revelations of the utmost importance to share, they think they've got one of the most crucial secrets to how the world works, they feel a constant need to impart it to you straightaway with an air of mystery and all the commentary that goes with it, those people who say I've got the answer so ask me a question, and with that they think they've become your guru, it's incredible how many people pretend to be serious, me I'm more of a deadpan type, if you know what I mean, so I get bored with long speeches, I prefer funny stories you can tell your friends around a table, there's no need to bring out the finest china every time you want to speak to someone, I like simple, direct words, you know, those words that you can tell come straight from the heart, I like people who aren't afraid to speak their minds, sincerity's really important, you can always tell whether you're dealing with someone sincere or a phrasemonger, when I've got something to say to someone I say it, point blank, there's no need for lots of digressions and roundabout talk, making a rigmarole of your phrases, gilding the lily with chocolate sauce, if I have nothing to say I keep quiet, it's important that some people know when to keep quiet, that we can do without all these useless declarations people are making a hundred times a day, all that wasted saliva, for nothing at all, just wind, for the pleasure of talking, making noise, you get the impression that some people think the more they talk the more personality they have, at the same time there's something fascinating about people who never stop talking, they use words as a feast, they go trundling through every nook and cranny of the language, when they speak it isn't for you, it's for themselves, it's smoking away inside them and it needs to come out, and also chatty people are often good-natured, whereas the silent types tend to be grumpy, I've always been frightened of taciturn people, silence is death, you see, I don't like people who can't say a word and are always asking you to be their spokesman, they cling to you like an ulcer and you end up speaking for two, you do all the work, this whole race of parasites and speech suckers is dangerous, I'm telling you, they're sly and hypocritical, they don't give you even a whiff of their real personalities, they use the trouble they have expressing themselves as an excuse to stay in the shade, although I should say I have a hard time dealing with those people who'd jump up in your face to tell you their life story in minute detail, to tell you their most personal secrets, you'd think these weirdos spent their whole lives in the confessional, personally I'm not that interested in other people's lives, first of all it's always the same, tales of hanky-panky, a happy or unhappy childhood with Mommy and Daddy, money trouble, garden trouble, moral trouble, it's crazy how boring other people's problems can be, and if you're lucky they don't also feel the need to tell you their dreams on top of it all, some people are specialists in this type of storytelling, you may note that if you want to get your listener interested in your dream all you have to do is say you dreamt about him, it never fails, you'll see him immediately get into the most receptive listening attitude, so to be nice you stick him in the corner somewhere in your dream and you've got a good audience for any story, however interminable, it's a nice feeling to have an audience that pays attention, doesn't interrupt all the time or get distracted, I hate people who always shout come to the point, come to the point, they seem to get in a rage and stamp their feet just because you're carefully laying out the preliminary details, in any case, if I'm telling a story I can't stand it when I suddenly get the impression my listener's not interested anymore, what's the point of striving to speak well if there's nothing but a void listening, that being said, I'm not too chatty myself, but still, once in a while I like to be able to tell my little story like anybody else, after all the reason we have a language is to use it, and some people are crazy about stories, they keep asking for more, and the more far-fetched stories you tell them, the more they believe them, the bigger the starship you paint for them, the more they start itching for an implausible journey, but it isn't easy to fool your listener, to lie well, to lie sensitively, if I can put it that way, there's an art to it, you have to be able to stand your listener in front of a mirror, then slip a second mirror between his face and the first one, and then another, and another, and you go on like that as long as you like and your victim keeps smiling sweetly at each new mirror, doesn't have a clue what's going on, but when you finally put the first mirror back, he screams in horror because he doesn't recognize himself, one sad autumn day they found poor Caracala's body in a ditch, he'd been killed, some coward had attacked him from behind, stuck a knife in his back, you have to admit it's a heinous act to attack someone like that, who can't defend himself, he couldn't even call for help, the whole village was in a state because we really liked our idiot, he had his place in our group, you see, and I'd taken him under my wing a long time ago, I gave him clothes I didn't wear anymore, made sure he always got something to eat, that he didn't suffer too much with life's hardships, well you can imagine how unfounded the rumors about this awful incident were, and although the police held me for lengthy questioning they were never able to prove a thing, in any case I always kept that to myself, even at the worst moments of my interrogation, and between you and me Marie-Ange was far from an innocent bystander in what happened, it was a hell of a coincidence that she spent so much time looking after Caracala in the days leading up to the murder, I happen to know personally that she didn't like that guy very much, and I'd like to tell you also that it wasn't her first piece of dirty work, you remember the fire at the Tabarin, I'd stake my life on her being involved in that weird story, which was never completely resolved, that girl was always kind of bizarre, you know, but I didn't want to say anything to the police, I felt she was young then and had her whole life ahead of her to redeem herself, I don't know what happened to her later, they said she went to work in town but I'd already lost contact with

her, it was better for us not to see each other much after that sad incident, especially because I didn't appreciate all the lies she told about
me, it was exactly as if she'd wanted to blame it all on me so I could
be the fall guy, I remember staying home for several days without
going out, it was good to spend some time in the warmth of our family home, I always got along really well with my parents, I did everything I could to be nice to them, I helped my mom do the house-
work, and a few months later I said to my dad, listen, if you want,
I'll come and work with you, his face was glowing with happiness,
the poor old guy was so glad to hear that, I really think that was the
happiest day of his life, I'd come to the decision because, after all,
you can't spend your whole life doing nothing, and I'd been interested in heating and chimneys ever since I was a child, sometimes
during vacation I'd go to work with my dad, I'd watch him, I ad-
mired his skill and thought to myself, I'd like to do that job someday,
it's a wonderful profession, you know, you're the one who helps people keep warm, they've got you to thank for all their lovely evenings
by the fire, and it brings you joy to know that, thanks to your work,
they're sitting there dreaming and watching the dancing flames, I
was still really young when my dad told me a dreadful story, there
was a guy who used to seduce honest ladies by dangling a happily
married future in front of them, he'd invite them to a villa in the
countryside and there'd be plenty of hanky-panky, at the same time
he'd make sure they'd give him a nice little loan, once he got the key
to the money-box he didn't waste a second, he'd bump them straight
off and burn them in the stove at the villa, well this guy ended up in
court, there was plenty of evidence that he was guilty but he always
denied it vehemently, he even had a wife and kids and everyone said
he loved his family, maybe the most interesting thing was that he
didn't take all the necessary precautions, for example out in the garden they found some small bone fragments in a pile of ash that came
from the stove, which indicated he hadn't made sure those bodies
were completely charred, down to the last sliver, but maybe it wasn't
his fault after all, maybe with the state of the stove he couldn't do any

better, you see lots of setups that don't work correctly, you know, in our line of work we see them every day, and it's true that my dad taught me his trade marvelously well, he was a worker like you used to still find in those days, it was in his blood, he lived for his heaters, he died not long after his retirement, he missed his fireplaces and chimneys too much, even if he stayed busy in the garden all day it wasn't enough to keep him interested, I'd built him a little shed to store his tools in by the cemetery wall, but the poor man hardly had time to use them, and the saddest part was that after he died, my mother couldn't find anything better to do than get together with Victor, and I'd told her if that guy moves in, I won't set foot in this house again, I knew him well, you see, he was a good-for-nothing idler, when it came to hanging out in bars, holding forth for hours on end, sure, he could do that, but as for work it was a whole different story, all those stories he told were nothing but a heap of lies, that old boy lied through his teeth, he lied just like breathing, in any case the only other thing he was capable of doing was sitting in the sun in front of his house with his dog lying next to him and playing a strange tune, always the same one, with the tiny flute he'd carved from a pigeon's bone!

Paul Emond was born in Brussels in 1944. After obtaining his doctorate at the University of Louvain, he spent three years in Czechoslovakia and wrote his first novel. Returning to Belgium, he worked for the Archives etMusée de la Littérature in Brussels, eventually becoming a professor at the Institut des Arts de Diffusion, where he teaches today. An accomplished dramatist as well as a fiction writer, Emond's first play debuted in 1986, with more than fifteen to follow, which have been performed in numerous countries around the world.

Marlon Jones has previously translated Louis-Ferdinand Céline and François Cusset. He lives in England with his wife and son.

MICHAL AJVAZ, *The Golden Age.*
    The Other City.

PIERRE ALBERT-BIROT, *Grabinoulor.*

YUZ ALESHKOVSKY, *Kangaroo.*

FELIPE ALFAU, *Chromos.*
    Locos.

IVAN ÂNGELO, *The Celebration.*
    The Tower of Glass.

ANTÓNIO LOBO ANTUNES,
    Knowledge of Hell.
    The Splendor of Portugal.

ALAIN MRIAS-MISSON, *Theatre of Incest.*

JOHN ASHBERY AND JAMES SCHUYLER,
    A Nest of Ninnies.

ROBERT ASHLEY, *Perfect Lives.*

GABRIELA AVIGUR-ROTEM,
    Heatwave and Crazy Birds.

DJUNA BARNES, *Ladies Almanack.*
    Ryder.

JOHN BARTH, *Letters.*
    Sabbatical.

DONALD BARTHELME, *The King.*
    Paradise.

SVETISLAV BASARA, *Chinese Letter.*

MIQUEL BAUÇÀ, *The Siege in the Room.*

RENÉ BELLETTO, *Dying.*

MAREK BIEŃCZYK, *Transparency.*

ANDREI BITOV, *Pushkin House.*

ANDREJ BLATNIK, *You Do Understand.*

LOUIS PAUL BOON, *Chapel Road.*
    My Little War.
    Summer in Termuren.

ROGER BOYLAN, *Killoyle.*

IGNÁCIO DE LOYOLA Brandāo,
    Anonymous Celebrity.
    Zero.

BONNIE BREMSER, *Troia: Mexican Memoirs.*

CHRISTINE BROOKE-ROSE,
    Amalgamemnon.

BRIGID BROPHY, *In Transit.*

GERALD L. BRUNS,
    Modern Poetry and the Idea of Language.

GABRIELLE BURTON, *Heartbreak Hotel.*

MICHEL BUTOR, *Degrees,*
    Mobile.

G. CABRERA INFANTE,
    Infante's Inferno.
    Three Trapped Tigers.

JULIETA CAMPMPOS,
    The Fear of Losing Eurydice.

ANNE CARSON, *Eros the Bittersweet.*

ORLY CASTEL-BLOOM, *Dolly City.*

LOUIS-FERDINAND CÉLINE,
    Castle to Castle.
    Conversations with Professor Y,
    London Bridge,
    Normance,
    North,
    Rigadoon.

MARIE CHAIX,
    The Laurels of Lake Constance.

HUGO CHARTERIS, *The Tide Is Right.*

ERIC CHEVILLARD, *Demolishing Nisard.*

MARC CHOLODENKO, *Mordechai Schamz.*

JOSHUA COHEN, *Witz.*

EMILY HOLMES COLEMAN,
    The Shutter of Snow.

ROBERT COOVER, *A Night at the Movies.*

STANLEY CRAWFORD, *Log of the S.S,*
    The Mrs Unguentine,
    Some Instructions to My Wife.

RENÉ CREVEL, PUTTING *My Foot in It.*

RALPH CUSACK, *Cadenza.*

NICHOLAS DELBANCO,
    The Count of Concord,
    Sherbrookes.

NIGEL DENNIS, *Cards of Identity.*

PETER DIMOCK,
    A Short Rhetoric for Leaving the Family.

ARIEL DORFMFMAN, *Konfidenz.*

FOR A FULL LIST OF PUBLICATIONS, VISIT: www.dalkeyarchive.com

⬚ SELECTED DALKEY ARCHIVE TITLES

COLEMAN DOWELL, *Island People,*
Too Much Flesh and Jabez.

ARKADII DRAGOMOSHCHENKO,
Dust.

RIKKI DUCORNET,
The Complete Butcher's Tales,
The Fountains of Neptune,
The Jade Cabinet,
Phosphor in Dreamland.

WILLIAM EASTLAKE, *The Bamboo Bed,*
Castle Keep,
Lyric of the Circle Heart.

JEAN ECHENOZ, *Chopin's Move.*

STANLEY ELKIN, *A Bad Man,*
Criers and Kibitzers, Kibitzers and Criers,
The Dick Gibson Show,
The Franchiser,
The Living End,
Mrs. Ted Bliss.

FRANÇOIS EMMMMANUEL,
Invitation to a Voyage.

SALVADOR ESPRIU,
Ariadne in the Grotesque Labyrinth.

LESLIE A. FIEDLER,
Love and Death in the American Novel.

JUAN FILLOY, *Op Oloop.*

ANDY FITCH, *Pop Poetics.*

GUSTAVE FLAUBERT,
Bouvard and Pécuchet.

KASS FLEISHER, *Talking out of School.*

FORD MADOX FORD,
The March of Literature.

JON FOSSE, *Aliss at the Fire,*
Melancholy.

MAX FRISCH, *I'm Not Stiller,*
Man in the Holocene.

CARLOS FUENTES, *Christopher Unborn,*
Distant Relations,
Terra Nostra,
Where the Air Is Clear.

TAKEHIKO FUKUNAGA,
Flowers of Grass.

WILLIAM GADDIS, *J R, The Recognitions.*

JANICE GALLOWAY, *Foreign Parts,*
The Trick Is to Keep Breathing.

WILLIAM H H. GASS,
Cartesian Sonata and Other Novellas,
Finding a Form,
A Temple of Texts,
The Tunnel,
Willie Masters' Lonesome Wife.

GÉRARD GAVARRY, *Hoppla! 1 2 3.*

ETIENNE GILSON,
The Arts of the Beautiful, Forms
and Substances in the Arts.

C. S S. GISCOMBE, *Giscome Road,*
Here.

DOUGLAS GLOVER,
Bad News of the Heart.

WITOLD GOMBROWICZ,
A Kind of Testament.

PAULO EMÍLIO SALES GOMES,
P's Three Women.

GEORGI GOSPODINOV, *Natural Novel.*

JUAN GOYTISOLO, *Count Julian,*
Juan the Landless,
Makbara,
Marks of Identity.

HENRY GREEN, *Back,*
Blindness,
Concluding,
Doting,
Nothing.

JACK GREEN, *Fire the Bastards!*

JIŘÍ GRUŠA, *The Questionnaire.*

MELA HARTWIG,
Am I a Redundant Human Being?

JOHN HAWKES, *The Passion Artist,*
Whistlejacket.

ELIŻABETH HEIGHWAY, ED.,
Contemporary Georgian Fiction.

ALEKSANDAR HEMON, ED.,
Best European Fiction.

AIDAN HIGGINS, *Balcony of Europe,*
  Blind Man's Bluff,
  Bornholm Night-Ferry,
  Flotsam and Jetsam,
  Langrishe, Go Down,
  Scenes from a Receding Past.

KEIZO HINO, *Isle of Dreams.*

KAZUSHI HOSAKA, *Plainsong.*

ALDOUS HUXLEY, *Antic Hay,*
  Crome Yellow,
  Point Counter Point,
  Those Barren Leaves,
  Time Must Have a Stop.

NAOYUKI II, *The Shadow of a Blue Cat.*

GERT JONKE, *The Distant Sound,*
  Geometric Regional Novel,
  Homage to Czerny,
  The System of Vienna.

JACQUES JOUET, *Mountain R,*
  Savage,
  Upstaged.

MIEKO KANAI, *The Word Book.*

YORAM KANIUK, *Life on Sandpaper.*

HUGH KENNER, Flaubert,
  Joyce and Beckett: The Stoic Comedians,
  Joyce's Voices.

DANILO KIS˘, *The Attic,*
  Garden, Ashes,
  The Lute and the Scars,
  Psalm 44,
  A Tomb for Boris Davidovich.

ANITA KONKKA, *A Fool's Paradise.*

GEORGE KONRÁD, *The City Builder.*

TADEUSZ KONWICKI,
  A Minor Apocalypse,
  The Polish Complex.

MENIS KOUMANDAREAS, *Koula.*

ELAINE KRAF, *The Princess of 72nd Street.*

JIM KRUSOE, *Iceland.*

AYŞE KULIN,
  Farewell: A Mansion in Occupied Istanbul.

EMILIO LASCANO TEGUI,
  On Elegance While Sleeping.

ERIC LAURRENT, *Do Not Touch.*

VIOLETTE LEDUC, *La Bâtarde.*

EDOUARD LEVÉ, *Autoportrait,*
  Suicide.

MARIO LEVI, *Istanbul Was a Fairy Tale.*

DEBORAH LEVY, *Billy and Girl.*

JOSE´ LEZAMA LIMA, *Paradiso.*

ROSA LIKSOM, *Dark Paradise.*

OSMAN LINS,
  Avalovara,
  The Queen of the Prisons of Greece.

ALF MAC LOCHLAINN, *T*
  he Corpus in the Library,
  Out of Focus.

RON LOEWINSOHN, *Magnetic Field(s).*

MINA LOY, *Stories and Essays of Mina Loy.*

D. KEITH MANO, *Take Five.*

MICHELINE AHARONIAN MARCOM,
  The Mirror in the Well.

BEN MARCUS, *The Age of Wire and String.*

WALLACE MARKFIELD, *Teitlebaum's*
  Window,
  To an Early Grave.

DAVID MARKSON, *Reader's Block,*
  Wittgenstein's Mistress.

CAROLE MASO, *AVA.*

LADISLAV MATEJKA &
KRYSTYNA POMORSKA, EDS.,
  Readings in Russian Poetics: Formalist and
  Structuralist Views.

HARRY MATHEWS, *Cigarettes,*
  The Conversions,
  The Human Country: New and Collected Stories,
  The Journalist,
  My Life in CIA,
  Singular Pleasures,
  The Sinking of the Odradek
  Stadium,
  Tlooth.

JOSEPH MCELROY,
  Night Soul and Other Stories.

☐ SELECTED DALKEY ARCHIVE TITLES

ABDELWAHAB MEDDEB, *Talismano.*

GERHARD MEIER, *Isle of the Dead.*

HERMAN MELVILLE, *The Confidence-Man.*

AMANDA MICHALOPOULOU, *I'd Like.*

STEVEN MILLHAUSER,
The Barnum Museum,
In the Penny Arcade.

RALPH J. MILLS, JR., *Essays on Poetry.*

MOMUS, *The Book of Jokes.*

CHRISTINE MONTALBETTI,
The Origin of Man,
Western.

OLIVE MOORE, *Spleen.*

NICHOLAS MOSLEY, *Accident,*
Assassins,
Catastrophe Practice,
Experience and Religion,
A Garden of Trees,
Hopeful Monsters,
Imago Bird,
Impossible Object,
Inventing God,
Judith,
Look at the Dark,
Natalie Natalia,
Serpent,
Time at War.

WARREN MOTTE, *Fables of the Novel: French*
Fiction since 1990,
Fiction Now: The French Novel in the 21st
Century,
Oulipo: A Primer of Potential Literature.

GERALD MURNANE, *Barley Patch,*
Inland.

YVES NAVARRE,
Our Share of Time,
Sweet Tooth.

DOROTHY NELSON, *In Night's City,*
Tar and Feathers.

ESHKOL NEVO, *Homesick.*

WILFRIDO D D. NOLLEDO,
But for the Lovers.

FLANN O'BRIEN, *At Swim-Two-Birds,*
The Best of Myles,
The Dalkey Archive,
The Hard Life,
The Poor Mouth,
The Third Policeman.

CLAUDE OLLIER, *The Mise-en-Scène,*
Wert and the Life Without End.

GIOVANNI ORELLI, *Walaschek's Dream.*

PATRIK OUŘEDNÍK, *Europeana,*
The Opportune Moment, 1855.

BORIS PAHOR, *Necropolis.*

FERNANDO DEL PASO,
News from the Empire,
Palinuro of Mexico.

ROBERT PINGET, *The Inquisitory,*
Mahu or The Material,
Trio.

MANUEL PUIG, *Betrayed by Rita Hayworth,*
The Buenos Aires Affair,
Heartbreak Tango.

RAYMYMOND QUENEAU, *The Last Days,*
Odile,
Pierrot Mon Ami,
Saint Glinglin.

ANN QUIN, *Berg,*
Passages,
Three,
Tripticks.

ISHMAEL REED, *The Free-Lance Pallbearers,*
The Last Days of Louisiana Red,
Ishmael Reed: The Plays,
Juice!,
Reckless Eyeballing,
The Terrible Threes,
The Terrible Twos,
Yellow Back Radio Broke-Down.

JASIA REICHARDT,
15 Journeys Warsaw to London.

NOËLLE REVAZ,
With the Animals.

JOÃO UBALDO RIBEIRO,
House of the Fortunate Buddhas.

JEAN RICARDOU, *Place Names.*

RAINER MARIA RILKE,
The Notebooks of Malte Laurids Brigge.

JULIÁN RÍOS, *The House of Ulysses,*
Larva: A Midsummer Night's Babel,
Poundemonium,
Procession of Shadows.

AUGUSTO ROA BASTOS, *I the Supreme.*

DANIËL ROBBERECHTS,
Arriving in Avignon.

JEAN ROLIN,
The Explosion of the Radiator Hose.

OLIVIER ROLIN, *Hotel Crystal.*

ALIX CLEO ROUBAUD, *Alix's Journal.*

JACQUES ROUBAUD,
The Form of a City Changes Faster, Alas,
Than the Human Heart,
The Great Fire of London,
Hortense in Exile,
Hortense Is Abducted,
The Loop,
Mathematics, The Plurality of Worlds of Lewis,
The Princess Hoppy,
Some Thing Black.

RAYMYMOND ROUSSEL,
Impressions of Africa.

VEDRANA RUDAN, *Night.*

STIG SÆTERBAKKEN, *Siamese, Self Control.*

LYDIE SALVAYRE, *The Company of Ghosts,*
The Lecture,
The Power of Flies.

LUIS RAFAEL SÁNCHEZ,
Macho Camacho's Beat.

SEVERO SARDUY, *Cobra & Maitreya.*

NATHALIE SARRAUTE,
Do You Hear Them?,
Martereau,
The Planetarium.

ARNO SCHMIDT, *Collected Novellas,*
Collected Stories,
Nobodaddy's Children,
Two Novels.

ASAF SCHURR, *Motti.*

GAIL SCOTT, *My Paris.*

DAMION SEARLS, *What We Were Doing and*
Where We Were Going.

JUNE AKERS SEESE,
Is This What Other Women Feel Too?,
What Waiting Really Means.

BERNARD SHARE, *Inish, Transit.*

VIKTOR SHKLOVSKY, *Bowstring,*
Knight's Move,
A Sentimental Journey: Memoirs 1917–1922,
Energy of Delusion: A Book on Plot,
Literature and Cinematography,
Theory of Prose,
Third Factory,
Zoo, or Letters Not about Love.

PIERRE SINIAC, *The Collaborators.*

KJERSTI A. SKOMSVOLD, *T*
he Faster I Walk, the Smaller I Am.

JOSEF S̆KVORECKÝ,
The Engineer of Human Souls.

GILBERT SORRENTINO,
Aberration of Starlight,
Blue Pastoral,
Crystal Vision,
Imaginative Qualities of Actual Things,
Mulligan Stew,
Pack of Lies,
Red the Fiend,
The Sky Changes,
Something Said,
Splendide-Hôtel,
Steelwork,
Under the Shadow.

W. M. SPACKMAN, *The Complete Fiction.*

ANDRZEJ STASIUK, *Dukla,*
Fado.

GERTRUDE STEIN, *The Making of Americans,*
A Novel of Thank You.

LARS SVENDSEN, *A Philosophy of Evil.*

PIOTR SZEWC, *Annihilation.*

GONÇALO M. TAVARES, *Jerusalem,*
Joseph Walser's Machine,
Learning to Pray in the Age of Technique.

FOR A FULL LIST OF PUBLICATIONS, VISIT: www.dalkeyarchive.com

LUCIAN DAN TEODOROVICI,
Our Circus Presents . . .

NIKANOR TERATOLOGEN,
Assisted Living.

STEFAN THEMERSON,
Hobson's Island,
The Mystery of the Sardine,
Tom Harris.

TAEKO TOMIOKA, *Building Waves.*

JOHN TOOMEY, *Sleepwalker.*

JEAN-PHILIPPPPE TOUSSAINT,
The Bathroom,
Camera,
Monsieur,
Reticence,
Running Away,
Self-Portrait Abroad,
Television,
The Truth about Marie.

DUMITRU TSEPENEAG,
Hotel Europa,
The Necessary Marriage,
Pigeon Post,
Vain Art of the Fugue.

ESTHER TUSQUETS,
Stranded.

DUBRAVKA UGRESIC,
Lend Me Your Character,
Thank You for Not Reading.

TOR ULVEN, *Replacement.*

MATI UNT,
Brecht at Night,
Diary of a Blood Donor,
Things in the Night.

ÁLVARO URIBE AND OLIVIA SEARS, EDS.,
Best of Contemporary Mexican Fiction.

ELOY URROZ, *Friction,*
The Obstacles.

LUISA VALENZUELA,
Dark Desires and the Others,
He Who Searches.

PAUL VERHAEGHEN,
Omega Minor.

AGLAJA VETERANYI,
Why the Child Is Cooking in the Polenta.

BORIS VIAN, *Heartsnatcher.*

LLORENÇ VILLALONGA, *The Dolls' Room.*

TOOMAS VINT, *An Unending Landscape.*

ORNELA VORPSI,
The Country Where No One Ever Dies.

AUSTRYN WAINHOUSE,
Hedyphagetica.

CURTIS WHITE,
America's Magic Mountain,
The Idea of Home,
Memories of My Father Watching TV,
Requiem.

DIANE WILLIAMS,
Excitability: Selected Stories, Romancer Erector.

DOUGLAS WOOLF,
Wall to Wall,
Ya! & John-Juan.

JAY WRIGHT,
Polynomials and Pollen,
The Presentable Art of Reading Absence.

PHILIP WYLIE, *Generation of Vipers.*

MARGUERITE YOUNG,
Angel in the Forest,
Miss MacIntosh, My Darling.

REYOUNG, *Unbabbling.*

VLADO Z˘ABOT, *The Succubus.*

ZORAN Z˘IVKOVIC´, *Hidden Camera.*

LOUIS ZUKOFSKY, *Collected Fiction.*

VITOMIL ZUPAN, *Minuet for Guitar.*

SCOTT ZWIREN, *God Head.*